PENNY JORDAN

bought with his name

D1173451

Harlequin Books

TORONTO • NEW YORK • LOS ANGELES • LONDON
AMSTERDAM • PARIS • SYDNEY • HAMBURG
STOCKHOLM • ATHENS • TOKYO • MILAN

Harlequin Presents first edition January 1983
ISBN 0-373-10562-2

Original hardcover edition published in 1982
by Mills & Boon Limited

CHAPTER ONE

THE party was very obviously in full swing when Genista pushed open the door to Greg Hardiman's flat. She had knocked on it several times, but the noise generated by the party had prevented anyone from hearing her. The living area of the flat seemed to be full of couples smooching around to the sensual strains of the music coming from the hi-fi system, and it was several seconds before Genista could find her host. When she did, he slid an arm round her slender waist, pressing her against him, smiling down into the perfect oval of her face. Her eyebrows rose mockingly and she moved slightly away. Greg had been drinking and retained his grasp of her waist.

'Well, well, look what the wind blew in,' he commented, eyeing her assessingly. 'I didn't think you were going to be able to make it, sweet. A little bird told me you were planning to work late tonight. Keeps you busy that boss of yours, doesn't he?'

'Someone has to earn the profits,' Genista reminded him dryly.

It was true; she had been going to work late, but Bob's wife Elaine had rung and asked him if he could go home earlier than planned, and finding herself at a loose end Genista had come to the party. Already she was regretting her decision. She had been away from the office on her annual holiday and had returned to find the place in an uproar.

'Come on. I'll introduce you around,' Greg told

her, interrupting her chain of thought. 'It isn't
often you grace our humble efforts at entertaining
with your presence. Pity I'm leaving for the States
at the end of the week. I've always fancied you,
Gen; wondered what goes on behind those cool
"keep your distance" barricades. I don't suppose
you feel like staying on when the others have
gone?'

Genista had heard the same question too often
before to feel shocked or angry. What was it about
men that made them calmly assume that any
woman who wasn't attached and over twenty-one
must automatically want to jump in and out of
their beds? She had been putting men like Greg
down for nearly four years, but still they had the
arrogance to think all they had to do was smile
and pay a few meaningless compliments for a girl
to be ready to sleep with them.

She moved away, refusing Greg's offer to introduce her around. She knew most of the people
present. Like her, they worked for Computerstore,
a small firm pioneering and selling advanced com-
puter softwear to industry and commerce. Genista
had been with them for four years—ever since she
had come to London, in fact, and she thoroughly
enjoyed her job as personal assistant to the firm's
Liaison Manager, or at least she had done up until
now. A small frown furrowed her brow as she
remembered the the news which had awaited her
return from Greece. Computerstore had been taken
over by a large organisation, and there were fears
within the firm that jobs would be lost; parent
company men brought in over the heads of existing
staff; people made redundant. Bob Norman, her own
boss had worn a perpetual frown all week. Genista
bit her lip. She was very fond of Bob. She liked

working for him very much. They made a good
team, and although she had taught herself not to
be emotional about other people she knew it would
be hard for her to work as well with someone else.

Collecting a drink from the makeshift bar, she
leaned against the wall, watching the antics of her
fellow-guests with a certain sardonic appreciation.
If she was any judge, a couple of promising affairs
would result from the forced hothouse atmosphere
of tonight's party; her lip curled faintly, although
she was unaware of it. She was by far the most
attractive woman in the room. Tall, slenderly elegant, her dark red hair curling on to her shoulders,
her features almost classically sculptured. It was
several seconds before her antennae warned her
that she was being watched. She didn't make the
mistake of looking straight away to see who was
watching her, but instead let her eyes drift casually
across the room.

He was leaning against the opposite wall, and
lifted his glass to her, in a salute which was partially
appreciative and wholly arrogant. With a sense of
mingled distaste and anger Genista realised that he
expected her to make her way across to him. He
was, she recognised, a man to whom women would
always run. Well, not this one. He was easily the
most striking man in the room. Even slouched
against the wall his body held an element of leashed
power more suggestive of the jungle than a small
London flat. He was dressed quite casually in black
cord jeans and a black cotton shirt, his thick dark
hair brushing the collar of his shirt at the back.

He must be in his thirties, Genista mused; far
too much aware of his sensual impact on suscepti-
ble females. He moved, easing his weight from one
leg to the other, the action tautening the powerful

thigh muscles beneath the cord. He was watching
her with hooded eyes. A pretty, dizzy young blonde
from the typing pool walked past him, eyeing him
provocatively. Silly little fool, Genista thought
pityingly. Couldn't she see he was way, way out of
her league, and if she played with him, she would
be badly hurt?

It did not occur to her to wonder who he was.
She felt no curiosity about his identity. She felt no
sense of pleasure because she had caught his eye.
She could read what was in his mind as easily as if
it were an open book. Had she responded to that
look he would have dated her a few times, and
would no doubt have expected to be repaid by
sharing her bed, and then when he grew tired of
her she would be quickly ditched while he moved
on to the next conquest. She watched the pretty
blonde typist trying desperately to catch his attention; he knew what the silly little thing was doing,
and although he acknowledged her efforts with a
faintly bored smile he made no attempt to spare
the girl the humiliation which would undoubtedly
be hers in the cold sober light of morning. He
looked across at Genista once again, and in that
look she read everything she most disliked about
his type of man; an arrogant assurance that she
was his for the taking, and all at once she was
filled with a desire to show him exactly how wrong
he was. As she smiled secretly and provocatively
into her half empty glass, knowing he thought the
smile was for him, she made up her mind that
before the evening was over she would humiliate
him to such an extent that he would never look at
any woman in quite such an arrogantly certain way
again.

She turned her back on him, walking casually

towards the window, to stand and stare out across the city. She was more simply dressed than the majority of the female guests, having come straight from the office, but the black top and silky wrap-around black and white patterned skirt she was wearing emphasised the tan she had got on Ionis. She loved the Greek islands, and Ionis most of all; hardly anyone went there. The beaches were small, and very private. She knew that the other girls in the office thought she was odd because she chose to take her holidays where she was unlikely to run into any men. She was staring up at the stars when she felt the hand on her arm.

'Full of dangerous allure, aren't they? So tantalisingly out of reach, drawing man to his doom, perhaps, like moths to the flame.'

She had seen his reflection in the glass as he came towards her, and now they were mirrored side by side, his height and breadth dwarfing her.

'You're an astronomer?' Her amethyst eyes betrayed nothing, but she allowed a hint of amused disbelief to colour the words. How easy it was to deceive men into seeing in a woman only what they wanted to see! She could tell that he thought she was flirting with him. How little he knew!

'Let's just say that while I'm attracted to dangerous and alluring things, I prefer them to be a little more within reach . . .'

His eyes were on her when he spoke, and although Genista smiled, inwardly she was thinking cynically, 'I'll bet! And I'll bet you don't like reaching very far for what you want either. Well, this time, my friend, while your greedy hands are stretching for the apple your feet will be taking you into quicksand.'

'Are you here on your own?'

He certainly believed in being direct, his eyes were on her ringless fingers, and Genista raised her eyebrows and smiled.

'If I'm not?'

He smiled, and for the first time Genista realised that his mouth was faintly cruel, turning down slightly at the corners; the mouth of a man who was unlikely to feel compassion for the weak.

'Then he's a fool for leaving something as beautiful as you on your own. And his loss is my gain!'

Genista had to bite hard on her tongue to prevent herself from commenting sharply on that 'something', but of course it was typical. He was obviously that type. His attitude was no more than she had expected. Hadn't she learned young that the male sex considered any girl attractive enough to warrant a second look fair game? Was he married? Somehow she did not think so. He didn't look married, although she admitted wryly that that was an irrational judgement. However, it would do no harm to make sure.

'And you?' she asked softly. 'Are you . . . alone?'

'Alone and unencumbered,' he confirmed, taking her arm. His fingers were hard and warm, curling round the tanned flesh of her upper arm. Despite her red hair she tanned well, and her skin had the colour and texture of a sun-ripened peach.

'Would you like to dance?'

She was going to refuse when she saw Greg heading for them. He had been making his desire for her very plain recently. She thought she had successfuly disguised her reactions from her companion when she allowed him to draw her into the dancers, but he surprised her by commenting urbanely as his arms slid round her waist.

'An ex-admirer?'

'More of a nuisance, really,' Genista, too surprised by his perception to contemplate lying, realised her mistake, when his eyebrows drew together slightly. How typical, was her annoyed reaction. No doubt he thought she had covertly encouraged Greg's attentions, secretly enjoying them. Men seemed to find it impossible to accept that a woman might not be interested in them. Well, he would learn.

'Relax!'

She hadn't realised how tense she had become, until his fingers stroked lightly along her spine. The action caught her off guard and she shivered with revulsion, thick, dark lashes masking her amethyst eyes.

Her companion had obviously taken her shudder for one of delight, for he pressed her closer to him so that her breasts were crushed against the black cotton shirt. She tried to move away, but his hands were spread out against her back. She could feel the warmth through her thin top.

'How about introducing ourselves? My name's Luke Ferguson. And yours?'

'Genista,' she told him briefly. She hated telling people too much about herself. It made them curious and they started to pry. It was a legacy from her schooldays when the other children had been inquisitive about her lack of a father. There was no slur on illegitimacy these days, but the old scars still ached.

'Genista! Pretty and unusual. Like its owner.'

'You find me unusual?' She was back on safer ground now—the accepted give and take of flirtation.

'You're right,' her companion drawled, pulling

her closer. 'Pretty is too tepid a description. You're an extremely beautiful woman, Genista, and I don't want to spend the rest of the evening sharing you.'

'What do you have in mind?'

Several people were watching them; in fact they had been the centre of a good deal of covert speculation as soon as they started to dance together. Genista could see Greg glowering at them from the kitchen door. She, personally had few doubts about what Luke had in mind; the same thing her father had had when he met her mother and Richard when. . . . But no, she was not going to think about Richard now. She would let her companion dig his own grave and then she would derive immense pleasure from watching him fall into it.

'If I told you, you'd probably have me certified. I think you're the most beautiful thing I've ever seen.' The hooded eyes were gleaming with a warmth which made Genista grateful for the fact that they weren't alone. Luke Ferguson was no callow boy, but a sophisticated male animal—and it showed.

'And for that I should have you locked up?' The verbal sparring was merely a prelude to the real purpose of the evening and she felt a tiny frisson of fear run down her spine when she saw the look in Luke's eyes. The desire burning there was real enough; too real, and just for a second, before dismissing the thought as pure imagination, she wondered if she had set a match to a fire she would be unable to control.

When the music stopped he released her reluctantly, and Genista let him slide his arm around her shoulders to pull her close to him as they left the floor. She was behaving in a way which was totally

out of character, but he did not know that. No
doubt he was used to women acquiescing eagerly
to his every suggestion. She was only surprised that
he hadn't already insisted that they went back to
his flat. He was in for a rude—and very public—
shock when he did, she told herself grimly. His
eyes, which had seemed almost black across the
width of the room were, in reality, very dark grey,
ringed with a slightly paler grey, and the desire she
could see smouldering in their depths seemed to be
his only vulnerability.

Greg came over to them, his arm draped round
the blonde typist Genista had seen watching Luke
earlier. Greg's eyes were faintly bloodshot and
Genista guessed that he had had too much to
drink.

'Well, well,' he drawled. 'What's all this? Has
our ice maiden melted at last? You *are* a lucky
man, Luke. Genista is one very choosy lady.'

'You've had too much to drink, Greg,' Luke told
him evenly. 'Why don't you take him away and
make him a cup of black coffee?' he suggested to
the blonde.

Quite a few people were watching them discreetly. Genista had been wondering how she
would deliver the body blow which would deflate
for all time Luke Ferguson's inflated ego, and all
at once she knew. He turned to her, his fingers
trailing down her cheek in a caress which parodied
tenderness, the desire burning in his eyes plain for
all to see.

'If you're ready to leave?'

He really was an excellent actor, she marvelled.
His voice had held just the merest suspicion of a faint
tremor, as though he were having great difficulty
in controlling his overwhelming desire to be alone

with her; as though he actually felt more for her than merely a fleeting need to assuage a momentary desire and reaffirm his belief in his irresistibility to her sex.

'Leave? With you?' She arched her eyebrows and managed a cool trill of laughter. 'My dear man, you've been entertaining company, but not that entertaining. I expect far more from a man than that before I allow him to take me anywhere.' She turned her back on him, and smiled at Greg. 'Be a darling, Greg, and get me another drink, will you?' He was too drunk to argue. Well aware that everyone was watching them, Genista turned back to Luke, almost as though the gesture were an afterthought, her expression mockingly bland as she suggested, 'If you're lonely why don't you ask Mary to go with you? You'd love Luke to take you home, wouldn't you, Mary?'

The blonde girl glowered angrily at her, ignoring Luke, as she tossed her head disdainfully.

'I'm not so short of a man that I need your cast-offs, thank you!'

Her departing flounce was rather spoiled by a slight wobble as she turned on excessively high heels, but otherwise her performance could not have been bettered had Genista written her script personally.

Luke was watching her with eyes that were suddenly smouldering like a volcano on the point of eruption, but Genista ignored the warning signs to say sweetly, 'Still here? Can't you take a hint?'

'That's what I thought I'd been doing ever since you walked in here,' he snarled back at her, all the earlier traces of pseudo-tenderness gone. 'You've been leading me on all evening, and now you turn me down flat. I want to know why, Genista.'

She hadn't been expecting this. She had thought that her refusal to leave with him would have been enough to make him disappear without another word.

'You do?' Somehow she managed to appear calm. 'Oh dear! I do so hate hurting people's feelings. You're a very attractive man, Luke,' she added sweetly, 'but you're just not my type.' She looked him up and down assessingly, a little surprised at her own ability to slip so easily into her new role. It was obviously true that there was a little of the actress in all women, although she seriously doubted her ability to give a repeat performance. Already her legs were beginning to feel distinctly shaky. There was something about the menacingly silent way in which Luke was regarding her that made her wonder if she might not have been wiser merely to have been satisfied with her initial success at putting him down, without trying to add any further gilding, but it was too late for second thoughts now. She had gone too far for those!

'Oh?' The solitary word was ominously quiet. 'When did you discover that fact? When I didn't accompany my offer to take you home with the promise of something more tangible if you spent the night with me?'

It was by a supreme effort of will that she prevented herself from hitting him. The cynical gleam in the charcoal grey eyes made the blood rush to her cheeks, but from somewhere she found the self-control to clench her hands into two small fists and say icily, 'There isn't enough money in the world to compensate me for having to endure a night in your bed. I can't think of anything that would fill me with more revulsion.'

'No?' Luke's voice had gone thick with rage. 'Then you're short of both imagination and memory. You were all but inviting me to make love to you there and then when we were dancing. If that was revulsion you felt you've got a damned funny way of showing it!'

When she didn't say anything his eyes suddenly darkened suspiciously, his fingers biting into her wrist as he grasped it, hauling her against him. 'You set me up, didn't you?' he demanded harshly. 'You deliberately led me on, fully intending to humiliate me, didn't you, you little bitch! God, you must be sick!'

Their onlookers had lost interest in them now and were drifting away. No doubt they thought Luke was still pleading with her to go with him, Genista thought wryly, nursing her aching wrist, when he turned without another word as he headed towards the door, leaving her standing alone.

'Phew, you were taking a bit of a risk, weren't you?' Jilly Holmes, Greg's secretary commented to Genista ten minutes later when Luke had gone.

Genista liked Jilly, they got on well together. She wrinkled her nose and shrugged. 'Serves him right. He shouldn't go round expecting females to fall at his feet with delight just because he deigns to smile at them.'

'You weren't exactly discouraging him, love,' Jilly pointed out mildly. 'In fact you were positively leading him on, and he didn't strike me as the type of man to take very kindly to the way you humiliated him. It was a bit much, wasn't it, Gen?'

'What are you trying to do? Stir up my non-existent conscience? I'm telling you, Jilly, he got exactly what he was asking for, supercilious brute!'

'Oh, come on. He was rather gorgeous. I wish he'd been looking at me the way he was looking at you. You had me convinced, you know. When the pair of you were dancing together, I thought the impossible had happened and you'd actually found a man you could like. You know, love, you were lucky he didn't get nasty with you. You were really giving him the green light.'

'Stop feeling sorry for him,' shrugged Genista. 'All I did was bruise his ego. You can't be foolish enough to think he cared about me. We'd only just met! All he wanted to do was get me into bed.'

'Don't be so sure. Haven't you ever heard of love at first sight?'

'Often, but not from anyone who's ever experienced it. Look, I think it's time I went. I don't know why I came really.'

'Umm,' mused Jilly. 'Well, you can't act the hermit all your life. I know you like to pretend that you're quite happy in your solitude, but there must be times when you feel . . .'

'A longing for a home and family?' Genista interrupted briskly. 'Never! Happy families are a myth, that's all. Say goodbye to Greg for me, will you, Jilly. I'm going now.'

'And you're going to walk, I suppose, all on your own through the streets of London at this hour of the night. You must be mad!'

'It's only a short walk—quite safe. Don't fuss. After all, I'm probably in far less danger walking home alone than I would have been if I'd accepted a lift from Luke.'

'Umm, but *that* type of danger I could get to enjoy,' Jilly drooled unrepentantly, but her eyes were clouded as she watched Genista go. There had been a look in Luke Ferguson's eyes when he left the party that made her feel uneasy for her friend.

Genista, oblivious to Jilly's concerned thoughts, collected her jacket from the bedroom where the coats had been left, adroitly fending off an amorous pass from one of the more junior members of the staff, as she reached past him to open the door. The night air felt cold, the street below the flat was deserted, and for a moment she considered going back inside and calling a taxi. The knowledge that it might be quite a while before she could get one made up her mind for her. It would only take her fifteen minutes or so to walk home. She had never felt at any risk in London before, it was silly to do so now just because of what Jilly had said.

Poor Jilly! She had obviously been quite smitten with Luke Ferguson. Genista shrugged. He deserved everything he had got. Disconcertingly she remembered the pressure of his hands on her back when they danced. He had held her close, making her feel every movement of his body as they swayed to the music, and knowing that apparent capitulation then would make her revenge seem all the sweeter, she had not objected to the way he had held her. She bit her lip, unconsciously worrying at it as she stepped outside. The street was deserted. Turning right, she walked briskly away from Greg's flat, her mind on the possible repercussions of the takeover of Computerstore and its effect on her. She had no real need to work for a living, but she enjoyed her job and would not wish to lose it.

She had walked several yards before she became aware of the soft purr of a car engine behind her. At first it did not alarm her; all the old houses along this road had been converted into flats, and the sound of a car slowing to a halt was nothing to get frightened about. Only the car wasn't stopping. It was crawling slowly and purposefully along behind her, keeping pace with her, the long, shiny bonnet just visible out of the corner of her eye.

Automatically she started to walk faster. Her mouth had gone terribly dry, fear tying her stomach into tight knots. Her heart was pounding, her legs trembling, as she prayed for a policeman to materialise and frighten off her pursuer. She had heard about girls being followed like this by men in cars, but it had never happened to her before.

She refused to glance at the car, or be panicked into any foolish action, and yet as the driver menacingly kept pace with her she found her eyes flickering nervously towards it, her heart coming into her mouth as she recognized the hard handsome profile of the driver. Luke Ferguson! He must have waited outside the flat until she left. Instead of reassuring her the knowledge of his identity increased her fear. She had never doubted that her behaviour had made him furious—that had been more than evident, and in view of his own arrogant attitude she had considered her actions completely justified, but now she was beginning to wonder how much she had underestimated him. He was following her to punish her; probably hoping to panic her into an ignominious flight which would be brought to an abrupt halt when it was outstripped by the powerful car he was driving. Up ahead of her an alleyway loomed, and with a feeling of relief she remembered that it led to a small square from which she could quite easily walk to her own apartment block. The alleyway was only a footpath; Luke could not follow her up it, and she hurried into it with a feeling of thankfulness, almost welcoming the darkness which swallowed her up as she stepped off the main road.

At first she was too relieved to have escaped to be aware of the soft footsteps shadowing the tapping of her high heels, and it was only some sixth sense that made her hesitate, nerves stretched like taut wire as her ears and eyes searched the darkness—no longer protective, but terrifyingly alien, masking all manner of danger. Nothing moved. She must have been imagining those faint sounds, Genista told herself. She turned, her sharp cry of protest cut off as strong fingers circled her throat.

'So you thought you'd eluded me, and now instead you find you've run straight into a trap' Luke jeered in a whisper. 'Oh, don't worry, I'm not going to harm you—much as I'd like to squeeze this soft throat of yours until you're begging me for mercy. Surely you didn't think I'd let you get away with humiliating me so easily?'

His grip of her throat prevented Genista from replying. Terror had given way to anger, and she struggled wildly, trying to free herself from the steel-like arm he had flung round her waist, pulling her back against him.

'When I walked in that room tonight and saw you, I thought I was seeing a dream. Your beauty caught me by the throat; there seemed to be an instant rapport between us, or so I thought. But I was wrong, wasn't I, Genista? All you saw was another man to build up and then let down. I've heard about women like you who get their kicks from that sort of thing.'

His grip on her throat had relaxed sufficiently for her to speak, her eyes mirroring her contempt as she stared up at him.

'Instant rapport?' Scorn laced the words. 'Oh,

come on. You can't expect me to believe that? I wasn't born yesterday, Luke. I know what men like you are looking for when they look at a woman. Someone who's accommodating in bed; someone who won't make a fuss when she's tossed aside to make room for the next in line. A little divertissement; a means of passing the time. You looked at me like a man who was trying to work out how long it would take you to get me into bed. Your vanity is so enormous that it never even occurred to you that I might not want to be there. You wanted me and that was enough. You deserved everything you got from me, Luke, so don't expect me to apologise. After all, I wasn't doing anything to you that you haven't probably already done to many, many women.'

'Is that a fact?' She could feel his body tighten with tension. 'I never argue with a lady.' He emphasised the last word, and Genista could feel the tightly leashed anger emanating from him—anger which he had no right to feel, she reminded herself. 'And contrary to what you seem to think, I've never gone in for physically humiliating them—until tonight.'

Before she could unravel the meaning hidden in the words he had spun her round, his arms locking tightly round her so that the palms of her hands were pressed against the hard warmth of his chest. He wasn't wearing a jacket and she could feel the crispness of his body hair beneath the thin cotton. Her mouth was dry with apprehension, perspiration breaking out over her body in a heated wave, despite the coolness of the evening.

'Let me go!' The words were betrayingly unsteady, and she knew from the satirical gleam of the cold grey eyes that she had not been able to hide her fear from him.

'This is for my own satisfaction,' Luke told her, as his head descended with slow deliberation. 'It's a pity no one else can witness it, but until I can find a way of getting public satisfaction for what you did to me tonight, it will have to do.'

What followed was like something out of a nightmare. His lips were cool; deceptively gentle at first, moving lightly against the numbed flesh of her own. Luke's weight bore her backwards, until she was leaning over his arm, her body vulnerably exposed to his eyes and hands—a situation of which he took full advantage as his free hand moved leisurely over her body, stopping nerve-rackingly just below the full curve of her breast, where her heart was beating like a trapped bird. It was a long time since a man had touched her so intimately. Richard had been the only one to do so—fumbled, uneasy caresses, nothing like the assured, knowledgeable touch of this man, who seemed to know instinctively the moment when her cool control would give way to deep shudders, which he mercilessly exploited, his hand sliding under the thin stuff of her top, pushing aside her bra to stroke her nipple roughly with his thumb.

When her mouth parted in shocked protest, his hardened over it, his kiss callously enforcing his superior strength. Bitter resentment filled Genista. What he was doing was tantamount to assault, and there was nothing she could do about it. The harsh pressure of his mouth was bruising the tender flesh of her lips, forcing them back against her teeth, with relentless, grinding pressure, his hand on her breast eliciting a response that shocked and humiliated. Since Richard no man had ever aroused her sexually; Richard she had loved and even with him she had been shy and reserved, and yet here was this contemptuous stranger, teaching her that her body was capable of a treachery she had never dreamed existed, because, despite her own horror and abhorrence, physically she had responded to him, and they both knew it.

When he released her, satisfaction gleamed in the steel-grey depths of his eyes, and childishly Genista rubbed the back of her hand against her mouth as though by doing so she could obliterate the memory of his touch. Where his hand had touched her breast it seemed to throb with an aroused awareness which awakened some deeply primitive core she had not known she possessed.

'My place or yours?'

The crude question brought her abruptly back to reality.

'Neither,' she said coldly. 'I meant what I said, Luke. I don't want you.'

'But I want you,' he said silkily, 'and you seem to have forgotten that this time I have the upper hand. You aren't surrounded by your friends this time, Genista. We're all alone here and there's no one to stop me forcing you into my car and taking you back to my apartment—and I will do if I have to, make no mistake about that.'

'You'd force me, merely to appease your masculine pride?' A little of her disgust must have showed in her voice, because for a second she saw something flicker in his eyes, and then they hardened.

'Why not? It might be quite an experience.'

'Meaning you don't normally have to use force, I suppose?' she said bitterly. She was feeling badly frightened, but she wasn't going to let it show.

'Not normally,' Luke agreed urbanely, but there

was a tightening of his mouth that warned her that
he was annoyed. 'As I say, it might be quite an
experience—for me. I doubt if you would enjoy it
very much. Not even an experienced woman enjoys
being raped.'

Raped? Genista stared at him.

'I'll report you to the police,' she said unsteadily.
'Rape is a criminal offence. You'll be thrown into
prison . . .'

'No way,' Luke told her cruelly, shaking his
head. 'Do you think after the way you were behaving at the party that any jury would believe you
weren't willing?—and I'd make sure they knew all
about it. You were leading me on. How old are
you? Twenty-four? Twenty-three? Old enough to
have had several previous lovers. That never goes
down well in court.'

It was a nightmare, Genista thought unsteadily.
This simple could not be happening, but it was,
and if she didn't go with Luke willingly now she
was quite sure that he would put his threats to
good effect. Rape! The word shivered horrifyingly
through her. Several previous lovers, Luke had
said. She bit back a hysterical laugh. She hadn't
even had one—Richard had seen to that! She took
a deep breath, her mind working overtime as she
tried to find a means of escape. She could always
run, but Luke would soon overtake her. Her brief
contact with his body had shown her that he was
lean and well muscled, more than a match for her!

'Well?'

'I'll come with you.' She took a deep breath and
tried to relax her tensed muscles. 'But it must be
my flat.'

She could feel him looking at her, trying to read
her mind. She held her breath, hoping he could not

guess what she had in mind.

'Very well,' he agreed slowly. 'Give me your doorkey. As a sign of good faith,' he mocked. 'I'm not having any doors slammed in my face this time, Genista, either metaphorically or actually.'

With shaking hands she opened her bag and removed her key. He took it in silence, his fingers biting painfully into her arm as he led the way back to his car.

It was a sleek dark red Maserati. Luke was obviously not short of money, Genista reflected as he opened the passenger door and waited until she was seated before closing it.

'Don't bother trying to open the door. I've locked it,' he told her sardonically, before walking round the car and sliding in beside her.

The confining interior of the car heightened her feeling of alarm. The upholstery was cream hide, the smell mingling with the sharply masculine fragrance of Luke's cologne. It was a masculine car, driven by a very masculine man, she thought, watching him change gear smoothly. The lights changed and they moved off with a smooth roar.

'Where do you live?'

She gave him directions automatically. If she hesitated and he took her to his own flat she dared not think of the consequences. What had started out as a simple exercise to show him that he simply could not have whatever he wanted, just because he wanted it, had turned into a nightmare of alarming proportions. The revenge Luke wanted to mete out in payment for the way she had humiliated him was something she could not endure, and would not have to endure if she was lucky. The hands resting lightly in her lap tensed, and she crossed her fingers childishly, uttering a silent prayer that the commissionaire of her apartment block would be in the foyer when they drove up.

She felt rather than saw the way Luke's eyebrows rose when she indicated that he should stop. The apartments had their own underground car park, but she wasn't going to direct him into that. Instead she let him pull up outside the discreetly expensive block, waiting passively for him to help her out of the car.

'You live here?'

The sharp enquiry heightened her fear.

'Yes.' She had bought her apartment when she first came to London. In many ways it had been a mistake, because the other occupants were mainly middle-aged couples, and apart from the occasional 'Good morning' or comments about the weather they had not exchanged any conversation.

The foyer was brightly lit from within, George sitting solidly behind his desk, and Genista felt a little of the tension drain out of her. He recognised her straight away, and started to smile as she walked in. Taking her courage in both hands, Genista turned to Luke, a false smile pinned to her lips.

'Thank you so much for a wonderful evening,' she told him, hoping that her voice did not sound as artificial to George as it did to her. 'I'll say goodnight now.'

For a moment she thought he was going to force a showdown. She could feel George watching them, and wondered feverishly if she should have pretended that he was accosting her in some way, and then just when she felt sure that her gamble had not paid off, she heard him say smoothly,

'Goodnight, Genista.' His hand slid from her

arm to her wrist, lifting her fingers to his lips and touching them with a panache that was making George goggle. 'You must think of our parting not as an end, but as a beginning.'

Genista could tell that George thought he was witnessing the tender beginning of a love affair, but beneath the lightly drawled words and the soft look she sensed an implied threat. Luke was warning her that he still intended to have his revenge!

Only when she was quite sure that the Maserati had pulled away did she turn towards the commissionaire, her voice shaky with released tension.

'George, I seem to have misplaced my key,' she told him. 'Would you be an angel and let me in? I think I'd better have the lock changed as well. You can't be too careful these days.'

'I'll see to it myself tomorrow, miss, if you like,' George offered. 'I'll just lock the main doors and then I'll come up with you and open your door for you.'

He'd always had a soft spot for her, right from the first day she moved into Mallory Court, he told his wife later. There was something about her. It wasn't just that she was beautiful. She made him feel all protective-like somehow. High time she got herself a boy-friend, he added, and by the looks of it the one she'd now found herself was doing alright for himself. Fast, powerful sports car . . .

Unware that she was the main topic of conversation in the commissionaire's flat, Genista prepared for bed. There were faint bruises on her throat, and she touched them lightly, shuddering. Jilly had warned her that Luke could be dangerous and she had laughed at her. She wasn't laughing now, and she was only thankful that it was extremely unlikely that she would ever see Luke

Ferguson again. First thing tomorrow she must remind George about changing her lock. When his anger cooled she doubted that Luke would pursue her any further, but she wouldn't be able to sleep in her bed at night knowing he had a key to her apartment. Her hand crept towards her breast. The flesh still tingled from his touch, emotions she had not experienced for years rushed through her, and she was remembering Richard. Luke ... Richard ... her father ... they were all the same. All men were the same; she turned her face into her pillow and allowed the frightened tears she had been bottling up from the moment Luke kissed her with such merciless contempt to flow freely at last.

CHAPTER TWO

GENISTA overslept—an almost unprecedented occurrence, and as she struggled to make her way to work through the crowded underground rightly or wrongly she blamed Luke Ferguson. He was the reason she had lain awake half the night, tormented by all manner of strange emotions. Forget the man, she told herself, stopping in her tracks so suddenly that the man walking behind her bumped into her, as she remembered that she had not seen George again about changing her locks. She bit her lip. She would have to try and ring through from the office. She didn't think Luke would try to use her key. He had struck her as a man of too much pride to attempt to see her again—unless his desire for revenge still burned as fiercely as it had done last night. She was being over-imaginative again, she told herself. It was over.

Bob was already seated at his desk when she walked in, his head bent over some papers. Computerstore was only a small concern; everyone worked together in one large office, except the owner and Managing Director, Brian Hargreaves, who was usually out somewhere selling the company's services. Since the news of their takeover had broken no one had seen Brian, although there were rumours that he had been offered a position on the board of their new owners. If that was the case they would need two new staff members; someone to replace Brian and someone to replace Greg, who had left the firm to take up a job in the States. Greg's loss did not particularly worry Genista. She could tolerate Greg, but she knew that beneath his surface charm lurked a particularly malicious streak which had often manifested itself in the manner in which he took her refusals to go out with him.

'Hello there! You're late!'

Jilly breezed into the office behind Genista, sighing enviously over Genista's pale lilac and cream separates. 'You always have such lovely clothes,' she complained. Jilly and her fiancé were saving up to get married and consequently there was very little money to spare for new clothes. Genista had bought her outfit from Jaeger—one of the benefits of having private means, she reflected wryly. No one could have been more surprised than Genista herself when, six months after the death of her parents in a landslide in the tiny Alpine village where they were spending their 'second honeymoon', she had received a letter from a firm of solicitors in Australia informing her that she was the sole beneficiary under the will of her mother's uncle. Genista had vague recollections of her mother talking about an uncle who had left England in disgrace, but she had never dreamed that he had built up a vast sheep station in the Australian Outback, which had been sold to his partner on his death, with the proceeds going to Genista as his only surviving relative. The money would keep her in modest luxury for the rest of her life, carefully invested, but she could not envisage life as a lady of leisure, so she had come to London, bought her apartment and set about finding herself a job which would fill the huge gap the death of her parents had left in her life.

'Hey, come back! Where were you? Having second thoughts about last night?' Jilly teased. 'So would I in your shoes. He was gorgeous—and very plainly fell hard for you. When he walked into the room and saw you he was almost transfixed—just like something out of the movies!'

Jilly was making her feel uncomfortable.

'It wasn't at all like that,' she protested. 'You're seeing things through rose-coloured glasses. All he wanted to do was go to bed with me. That's all men like him ever want.'

'If you believe that then you're the one with eye trouble—like you're wearing blinkers,' Jilly retorted spiritedly. 'Honestly, Gen, I sometimes don't think you're for real! The most gorgeous male I've ever seen in my life walks into a party, takes one look at you and gives a pretty fair impression of a man who's met the love of his life, and all you can do is say that he wanted to go to bed with you. You haven't the faintest idea! If that was all he wanted, why didn't he accept the invitation Mary was offering so blatantly?'

'Perhaps he prefers redheads,' Genista said flippantly. Jilly was being absurd. People in love were notorious for it. So she thought Luke had fallen for her, did she? *She* hadn't noticed!

'Who was he anyway?' Jilly asked. 'I've never seen him around before, have you, and most of the others were the usual crowd.'

'I've no idea,' Genista admitted. 'We didn't get as far as exchanging life stories.' She had no intention of telling Jilly what had happened after she had left the party; Jilly's questions awakened her own curiosity. Luke had come to the party alone, and had plainly not known many of the other guests. If it hadn't been for his air of arrogant command, and the powerfully expensive Maserati he had driven she might have put him down as one of Greg's ex-university friends; or someone who lived in the same block, but now that she thought about it, there had been an air of aloofness about Luke; a sort of aloneness, which didn't tie in with his being one of Greg's gregarious friends.

'I don't suppose you exchanged phone numbers?' Jilly pressed wistfully, plainly convinced that her friend ought to have encouraged Luke's attentions.

'No.' Genista purposefully made the word sound final, although a tiny part of her mind wondered what Jilly would have said had she told her that Luke did have her key.

'Join me for lunch?' Jilly questioned.

'I'll try. We might have to work through. Bob wanted to work late last night, but he had to go home.' A small frown furrowed Genista's forehead. She glanced across to where Bob Myers was still bent over his papers. He hadn't seemed his normal calm self after he had spoken to his wife the previous evening, and Genista hoped there was nothing wrong at home. Elaine was a charming person, although very much lacking in self-confidence. She and Bob had one son who attended a small public school, and privately Genista thought it was wrong that Elaine should live so much through her husband and son, although of course it was none of her business.

Bob smiled at Genista when she sat down at her own desk.

'Sorry I'm late. I overslept, and then Jilly collared me to chat about last night's party,' she apologised.

'So I saw,' said Bob with a smile. 'Don't let it worry you. Oh, by the way,' he added almost as though it were an afterthought, 'I've heard that our new boss is going to pay us a visit this morning. He rang me at home last night. He was hoping to get back from Amsterdam in time to do the honours, but there's been a hold-up with the Van der Walle deal.'

'Do you know much about our new owner?' Genista asked him, abandoning the chart she had been studying.

Bob shook his head. He was a tall, well-made man, still very attractive, his dark hair tinged with silver, a twinkle in his blue eyes as he studied Genista's downbent head. His manner towards her was fatherly, teasing almost, and Genista was able to enjoy his company without worrying that he might think she was attracted to him—Bob was very happily married; one of the very few who were, Genista often thought.

'All kinds of rumours were floating about while you were away,' he told her, 'but nothing concrete. The entrepreneur who built up the L.F.N. Corporation is something of a mystery man, apparently, and doesn't go in for publicity. Greg's met him. He called round at Brian's flat when he was there.'

'And promptly found himself a new job,' Genista commented dryly. 'Hardly a good omen.'

'Oh, you know Greg—or you should do by now. An easy life and a lavish expenses account and he was happy. I suspect when he heard the firm was being taken over he saw the writing on the wall. Brian Hargreaves is an excellent man in his field, but as an administrator he's inclined to be a little lax.'

Genista knew that this was true. Computerstore had a good reputation and did very well, but it could have done even better with tighter financial control, and certain members of the staff had very light duties in proportion to their generous salaries.

'You've no need to worry,' Bob assured her, as though he had read her mind. 'You're a very able worker, Gen, and there's no way I could manage without you.'

His phone rang, and Genista moved away as she heard him say sharply. 'Elaine!'

It was unusual for his wife to ring him at work, and she wondered again if something was wrong at home. Although they worked closely together and she had met Elaine, Bob was inclined to keep his private life private, and Genista had no wish to pry. She busied herself with her own work, which had piled up during her holiday, and when a sudden disturbance by the main door broke her concentration she glanced at her watch, surprised to see that the morning was almost gone.

Out of the corner of her eye she saw Bob leave his desk, and rather than appear curious she bent

her head over her own work again, even though
she had guessed that the disturbance had been
caused by the arrival of their new boss. No doubt
Simon, their commissionaire, had shown him up
from their reception area. Genista could hear the
familiar sound of Bob's voice; his introduction as
he paused by the desk used by the technical sales
team. Her desk was next in line, and it was very
tempting to glance up while the newcomer was
talking and snatch a quick look at him, but Genista
fought the temptation, and was glad that she had
done when he and Bob moved away from the tech-
nicians after a very brief exchange of conversation,
and walked towards her.

'Now let me introduce you to Gen, my assistant,'
she heard Bob saying. 'She's a real asset to the
firm. A hard worker . . .'

'Yes, I've already heard a great deal about
Jennifer.'

Genista felt as though someone had just poured
ice-cold water down her spine. She would have
recognised that voice anywhere!

'Jennifer?' she heard Bob say in a puzzled voice.
'Oh, I see! No, the Gen is short for Genista, not
Jennifer. I suppose really it's a crime to shorten
such a beautiful name.'

'Genista!' There was no discernible inflection in
the cool male voice as he repeated her name.
Genista had been staring at the faint stripe of
darker grey running across his pale grey tie while
he spoke, but now she lifted her eyes from the tie
to the cool grey eyes which almost matched it, her
stomach lurching betrayingly, despite the fact that
she had recognised his voice the moment she had
heard him speak.

'Genista!'

He held out his hand and she had no option but to place her own in it. In an immaculately tailored pale grey mohair suit and a fine silk shirt he looked very different from the man in black shirt and jeans who had pursued her down that narrow alleyway and kissed her so fiercely against her will, but he and this cool imposing stranger whom Bob was introducing as Luke Ferguson, head of the L.F.N. Corporation, were undeniably one and the same person.

She met his eyes as bravely as she could, and saw instantly that his shock had been as great as hers. Greg had known who he was, she remembered bitterly, and had no doubt enjoyed watching her put her career at risk. Well, he could fire her if he liked. In fact it would probably be better if he did, because there was no way she could continue to work for Computerstore if it meant that by doing so it would bring her into contact with him!

'So you're Bob's assistant?'

There was an odd inflection to the way he said the words; a look in his eyes that sent a frisson of alarm feathering down Genista's spine. Her chin lifted automatically, her eyes defying him to say what he was thinking.

'Do I get the impression you two already know one another?' Bob commented, obviously puzzled. 'But, Gen, this morning . . .'

'I didn't realise that Mr Ferguson was to be our new boss,' she interrupted coolly before Bob could complete his sentence. Faint colour burned up under her skin as she remembered the way she had deliberately set out to humiliate Luke the previous evening. Most of the other guests at the party had been on the staff of Computerstore. It wouldn't be

long before the news of their new boss's identity
got round; no doubt her colleagues were already
taking bets on how long it would be before she got
the sack. She would hand in her notice, she decided
wildly. The moment Luke had gone she would tell
Bob. The phone rang, cutting across her thoughts,
and she reached for the receiver automatically, only
to find Luke's lean fingers already clamped round
it. He lifted it to his ear, his expression sardonic as
he passed it over to her.

'For you. One of the hazards of employing a
beautiful woman, I suppose—her phone never
stops ringing!'

Genista could have told him that she never had
private calls at the office, but instead she took the
receiver from it him. The call was from the sales
manager of the garage from whom she had ordered
her new car. She had been promised delivery
several weeks previously, and the car had not
materialised. Now it had, and he wanted to know
when she wanted to pick it up. She bit her lip as
she hung up. Luke had turned aside to talk to Jilly,
who, despite her engaged state, was sparkling
prettily up at him, and under cover of their conversation managed to attract Bob's attention.

'Are you doing anything at lunchtime?' she asked
him quietly, but obviously not quietly enough.
Luke Ferguson must have ears like a bat, she
thought resentfully, as he turned smoothly from
Jilly back to Bob. 'I'm sorry, Bob, I forgot to mention it, but I've arranged for you to have lunch
with my personal assistant. He wants to talk over
several plans we have for streamlining some of your
systems, and I'm afraid we can't put it off because
he's due to fly north tomorrow to Aberdeen for
talks with one of the oil companies. There could be

a good contract in it for Computerstore, so I don't want to delay these talks. Sorry if it means putting off something important.'

He wasn't sorry at all, Genista thought angrily. She was quite sure he had just concocted that lunch just to obstruct her.

'Oh, not at all,' Bob said easily. 'It wasn't something that can't wait, was it, Gen? What did you want?' he teased with a grin. 'Surely not my advice on a new dress?'

Genista shook her head, wondering a little at the anger which suddenly seemed to burn in the dark grey eyes watching her so closely. 'It'll keep. I'll tell you about it later.' She had wanted Bob to go with her when she went to pick up her car. She was a little nervous about the thought of driving it for the first time in the lunchtime traffic, but she could ring the garage when he and Luke had gone and put them off until tomorrow.

'I don't suppose I would do in substitution?' Luke drawled, thoroughly disconcerting her. 'Since I've deprived you of Bob's company, offering my own instead seems a pretty fair recompense.'

'Do you think so?' Genista knew that Bob was frowning over her uncharacteristic behaviour. Jilly's mouth had fallen wide open, and Genista suspected that once they were alone the other girl would deliver another lecture, but right now she did not care.

'You'll have to forgive me, Mr Ferguson,' she added with a sweet smile, and the rather euphoric feeling that she was about to burn her boats with a vengeance, 'but I'm afraid there's simply no way you could stand in for Bob.'

It was a good exit line and she made the most of it, picking up her bag and walking swiftly towards the door before anyone else could add anything. It was lunchtime anyway, and she needed to be somewhere on her own to give herself time to recover from the shock of discovering that the new owner of the firm she worked for was none other than the man she had so grossly humiliated the previous evening. Damn Greg! He might have warned her! No doubt he had found it highly amusing. She should have remembered that he enjoyed playing tricks like that, and right from the start there had been something about Luke which had set him apart from the normal run of Greg's friends, despite his casual attire. Greg could be as vindictive as the most shallow-minded women on occasions, and it was Genista's misfortune that she had made her contempt of him too plain, too often.

She couldn't eat any lunch. She picked at a sandwich and drank half a cup of coffee before returning to the office. She had expected to find it deserted, but someone was standing by her desk, and her heart missed a beat as she recognised Luke's darkly handsome features. He had been bending over studying something, but as though he sensed her presence he stood up, his palm open, something glittering metallically on it.

'I thought I'd better not give you this while any one else was around,' he said softly, 'Although perhaps I'd be doing him a favour I doubt he'd continue to support you for much longer, once he knew that he wasn't the only one with a key to your rather expensive apartment. How does he manage it?' His eyes rested contemptuously on Genista's expensive separates. 'You don't strike me as a girl with exactly modest tastes—good clothes, an apartment in a luxurious block; discreetly expensive jewellery, in fact all the trappings of a young lady of some means. And he has a wife and child to keep as well, but then I suppose when it comes to a woman as beautiful as you a man will always find the necessary, won't he, Genista?'

Genista was too stunned to speak. For a moment she thought she must have misunderstood. Luke couldn't be suggesting that she was Bob's mistress, and worse still, that he was actually keeping her? But he was, as he soon made very plain.

'If you're thinking of denying it, don't bother. Greg told me all about you, but as he kept referring to you as "Jen", I thought your name was Jennifer. I ought to have known better. I'm renowned for my astute perception; that's how I got where I am today. I knew the first moment I saw you you weren't an ordinary run-of-the-mill girl, but I allowed my desire to cloud my judgment. No wonder you wouldn't let me take you home! You're a shrewd little bitch, aren't you? Why did you encourage me in the first place, Genista, or can I guess? Perhaps you'd heard that I'm a very rich man, and you got ambitious. If a man like Bob Myers will keep you so comfortably, think what I could give you? But you got cold feet, didn't you? You decided it might be better to be safe than sorry; after all, you'd no guarantee that I would give you anything, and you might lose Bob. You should have had more courage, my dear,' he told her softly. 'The way I wanted you last night. I'd have given you anything. However, the cold light of morning brings back sanity, so perhaps you made the right decision after all. Does Bob know about last night?'

'What is there *to* know?' Genista was amazed that she could sound so calm; that she could re-

spond so carelessly, when her furious repudiation
of his vile accusations had lodged like a hard ball
in her chest.

'What indeed?' Luke agreed silkily. 'But then
lovers are notoriously jealous people, and I still
have this.' He dangled the key from his fingers,
smiling cruelly. 'It would be the easiest thing in
the world for me to—er—remove it from my
pocket by mistake in Bob's presence, and the hardest for you to convince him that my possession of
it doesn't go hand in glove with my possession of
you.'

It was those last few words that did it, driving
from her the last vestiges of self-control, her hands
balled into two angry fists, as she turned to him,
angry colour burning up under her skin.

'I'd rather die than let you touch me, never mind
possess me!' Her voice was shaking with the pent-
up force of her anger. She was far too wound up
to be aware of the red tide sweeping under Luke's
own skin, or the rage burning blackly in his eyes,
all her attention concentrated on showing him in
what contempt she held him—his meaningless
threats, and his total misconception of her relationship with Bob. It was typical of a man like him
to leap to such a conclusion, she thought in disgust.
No doubt he had enjoyed the sort of relationship
he had accused her of having with Bob, with
countless numbers of women. It must be far easier
to rid oneself of them when one grew bored, if they
had merely been 'bought'. Well, no man would ever
buy her! Love was the only possible reason for
permitting a man sexual intimacy, and she already
knew to her cost that such an emotion simply did
not exist, and if that meant that she must go
through the rest of her life alone, then that was

what she would do. A kept woman! Her mouth
turned downward in a bitter grimace.

'So you'd rather die, would you?' The low,
almost snarled words held a dangerous threat, but
Genista was oblivious to it. Her face was paper-
white, her eyes as dark as pansies within its white
triangle. No man had ever spoken to her the way
Luke Ferguson had just done, and the shock of his
accusations had almost frozen her ability to defend
herself.

'And what about Bob's wife? Or doesn't she
come into your coldhearted calculations?' Luke
continued in obvious disgust. 'Don't you care that
you're breaking up her marriage—stealing her
husband?'

It was on the tip of Genista's tongue to tell him
that far from stealing another woman's husband,
she had always made a rule of avoiding any man
who she knew to be involved with another woman.
She had been too hurt by a man's duplicity once
before to risk the same sort of pain again.

'At least he isn't completely under your thumb,'
Luke added abrasively. 'Otherwise he'd be sharing
that apartment with you.'

His bitter contempt; the insults he was heaping
upon her combined to make her say recklessly,

'Perhaps I don't want him to. Perhaps I . . .'

'Perhaps you value your freedom too much to
give it up for any man,' Luke interrupted cuttingly.
'That's the sort of woman you are, isn't it, Genista?
Using your beauty like a weapon, always taking
and never giving. What happens when you grow
tired of Bob? Or was that what last night was really
all about? Are you already searching for his suc-
cessor?'

This time Genista's self-control snapped completely. The imprint of her fingers against Luke's lean tanned cheek took a long time to fade, through white to red, and then brown again, and during those seemingly endless moments, he neither spoke nor moved, but the look in his eyes spoke volumes.

She had behaved like a harpy, Genista thought wretchedly. What on earth had come over her? She prided herself on her cool control. Not even Richard, whose actions and words had surely been far more hurtful than Luke Ferguson's contempt, had provoked her to violence. A terrible nausea rose up inside her as she stared at the marks of her fingers against Luke's skin. Her legs seemed to turn to jelly, and she groped blindly for a chair.

'You're wrong. I . . .'

Her husky attempt at explanation and apology was swept aside.

'No, you're the one who's wrong, Genista, if you think you can treat me the way you have done and get away with it.'

As though the scales had suddenly been wrenched from her eyes, she saw him for the first time as the man he was; a man who had built up a multi-million pound financial empire virtually from nothing; a man notorious in business circles for his single-minded determination when it came to getting his own way; a man whom she had grossly humiliated and insulted, and who was now towering above her menacingly . . . a man with whom she was completely alone . . .

She stepped backwards on legs that trembled, longing to run, but mesmerised like a petrified rabbit by the dark grey eyes.

'Not so valiant now, are we?' Luke asked softly, moving as stealthily as a jungle cat.

Terror swept her, drawing her down into a black

vortex, paralysing her limbs completely.

'Oh no,' he continued in that same frighteningly steady voice, 'I'm not going to touch you now, Genista. But one day I shall. I fully intend to make you pay for last time, to honour the promises you made me albeit only with your eyes and body.' His mouth twisted in a cynical smile. 'And don't try to pretend that you didn't. You were taking me for a ride, Genista, but now I'm in control of the train and the ride won't be over until I say so.'

He was playing with her like a cat with a mouse, Genista thought bitterly, deliberately tormenting her, knowing that because she was his employee he had a certain amount of power over her.

'You don't strike me as a man who would compete for any woman,' she said bravely, trying to appear unconcerned. 'Especially one he knows to be the mistress of someone else.'

For a moment she thought he was going to strike her. Her body stiffened in fear, and his eyes gleamed satirically, the bitter hunger she had thought she saw there seconds before vanished so completely that she thought it must have been a trick of the light.

'I'm a businessman,' he reminded her coolly, 'and I don't like being cheated out of my just rewards. I wanted you the moment I saw you, Genista—you're a very beautiful woman—and I fully intend to have you!'

With that calm declaration he turned on his heel, leaving her alone in the office trying to come to terms with her chaotic thoughts. The man was unbelievable—insane even! He was behaving as though he were a feudal baron with rights of *droit du seigneur* over her. She knew she had every right to feel furiously angry, but for some reason the confrontation with him seemed to have drained her of the energy to feel anything apart from a panicky fear that stuck in her throat, causing her heart to beat nervously as she contemplated the words he had thrown at her before leaving the room.

Her fingers trembled as she dialled the foyer number of the flats. George answered almost immediatedly, assuring her that he had changed her lock. It must be the relief that made her feel so close to tears, she decided when she hung up, because certainly it was not like her to be so emotional.

When Bob returned from lunch she asked him if he could spare the time to accompany her to her garage.

'I'm terrified of driving the car for the first time,' she admitted to him ruefully, 'and I badly need some moral support.'

'You should have asked our new boss,' Jilly interrupted with a grin. 'He's really smitten, didn't you think so, Bob?'

'Don't be so ridiculous, Jilly!' Genista cut in before Bob could speak. 'I've already told you, you've got romance on the brain!'

'All right, tell me about your new car instead,' Jilly temporised. 'What make is it?'

'A Mercedes,' Genista told her, reluctant to sound as though she were bragging about her new possession. 'It's something I've wanted for a long time, and at last I've decided to take the plunge. It's a convertible—a sort of sports model, and I want Bob to come with me to pick it up. I'm terrified of driving it for the first time.'

'A Mercedes?' Jilly squeaked, in obvious awe. 'You lucky thing!' She said it without any malice, adding with a grin, 'A sports car too—what happens in the winter?'

Neither of them had seen Luke walk into the

room, and feeling relieved that her friend had exhibited no envy, Genista replied with a touch of slightly dry humour,

'Oh, I'll use the Ferrari then, of course. What do you think, Bob? When we've collected the Mercedes, how about buying a Ferrari?'

They were all laughing when Genista turned round and caught sight of Luke's openly contemptuous expression. Shock and guilt mingled on her own face, and it wasn't until much later that she realised he must have read in her expression confirmation of his suspicions that Bob was buying the car for her.

Bob's phone rang and Jilly drifted back to her desk, leaving Genista completely unprotected when Luke walked up and muttered in a voice which only carried as far as her,

'Perhaps I ought to start checking the books. There's no way Bob can afford the sort of luxuries that you demand, unless he's got private means. You certainly believe in pricing yourself high, don't you?'

'Meaning you couldn't afford me?' Genista parried swiftly, not caring what conclusions he would draw from her words. He already suspected the very worst it was possible for a man to think of a woman about her; any further conclusions he might draw could only be an anti-climax.

'On the contrary,' he told her smoothly, with a speed which caught her off guard, 'I could easily provide you with the Mercedes and the Ferrari. Think about it, Genista. I'm not averse to paying generously for my pleasures.'

'How predictable you are!' Genista hissed back angrily. 'You want something and you immediately think all you have to do is buy it. Haven't you learned yet that some things simply can't be bought?'

Her heated speech made him raise an eyebrow,

his eyes gleaming sardonically as he looked down at her, saying with slow deliberation, 'But we already know that you're not one of them, don't we, Genista?'

CHAPTER THREE

BOB and Genista left the office early, heading for the garage. The car was all ready for her. Bob and the salesman enthused over it, while Genista eyed the gleaming metallic green paintwork, and wondered how she had ever imagined she was going to be able to drive this elegant monster.

'It's a doddle really,' the salesman assured her. 'Automatic transmission—a beautifully well-behaved car, perfect for a beautiful lady,' he told her gallantly.

Bob was endlessly patient while Genista drove nervously towards her flat. He had an hour to spare, he told her, so if she liked they could drive about so that she could accustom herself to the feel of the vehicle.

By the time they returned to the apartment Genista was beginning to feel slightly more confident. The car, despite its weight and size, was easy to handle. The leather seats cushioned her comfortably, and there was plenty of space for her long legs.

'Can I reward your patience and steady your nerves with a drink?' she invited Bob when they stopped.

He glanced at his watch, the worry she had noticed earlier in the day in his eyes again.

'I won't, if you don't mind, Gen,' he apologised.

'It's Elaine. She's in a bit of a state.' He tugged uncomfortably at his tie, avoiding Genista's eyes, and then said on a rush, 'She's got some bee in her bonnet about getting old, says she's worried I might fall for some young dolly bird. I've told her it's all nonsense.' His voice had gone very gruff, and Genista's heart went out to both him and Elaine. 'Thing is, Gen, she's discovered a lump in her . . . in her breast, and she's working herself up into a rare old state about it. Our doctor's told her the chances are it will be benign, but she's convinced it will mean an operation . . .'

'Oh, poor Elaine!' Genista was genuinely sympathetic. How dreadful it must be for any woman to have to face that sort of operation, especially one as vulnerable as Elaine. No wonder she was worrying that Bob would find her less attractive! It was all nonsense, of course. Bob loved his wife, Genista knew that, but even so, she could quite see why he might not want Elaine to be unduly upset. Cold fingers of fear touched her spine. What if by accident Elaine should get to hear of Luke Ferguson's suspicions? But of course that was impossible. How could she? And suspicions were all that they were. Everyone else in the office knew that there was nothing between Bob and herself, and if Luke Ferguson bothered to ask around, he could find that out for himself.

When Bob had gone Genista ate a solitary meal, occasionally walking to the large window of her elegant living room to stare out in mingled fear and delight at her new purchase. George had been up with her new keys. He had seen her arrive in the car, and had made extremely approving noises, offering to garage it for her if she liked.

When she had finished her meal and washed up,

Genista turned on the television. The programme was a documentary about rural life in England, and to her amazement one of the villages featured was the one in which she had been brought up. As she listened to the presenter talking about the contrast between urban and rural life, her eye was caught by the man standing behind him in the small village square, and her heart started to pound heavily in recognition. It was Richard. An older Richard, of course, but still undeniably Richard with his handsome fair-haired good looks and well built masculine frame. Genista looked in vain for Elizabeth at his side, but then of course the daughter of the local landowner and M.P. was hardly likely to be seen frequenting a very ordinary village pub, which was what the television reporter had been doing before walking outside to talk about the experience, and Middle Hesford's pub was a real village pub, as Genista remembered, with no pretensions to fashionability. The local farm workers gathered there. Genista had only been once – with Richard. Their first date. She could remember it as clearly as though it had been yesterday.

She had lived in the village all her life, but for reasons which did not become clear to Genista until later, her parents had always kept themselves very much to themselves. Her father was a solicitor with a small practice in a nearby town. She was an only child, and her mother seemed to have no friends. Her parents were really all in all to each other, and often, without meaning to, they made her feel slightly as though she were in the way. Such love was very rare, as she had come to appreciate in the years since their death.

She had met Richard when he had come to seek

her father's advice about the purchase of a field adjacent to his farm.

Richard's father had owned one of the most profitable farms in the area, and following his death from a heart attack when Richard was still at agricultural college, the latter had returned home to take his father's place.

Richard's mother and two sisters lived with him. Genista knew him by sight. He was something of a local pin-up, and Genista, who had just left school, and was working in her father's office as a trainee secretary, had been overwhelmed when Richard had turned almost casually as she opened the door to let him out of the house, following his chat with her father, and asked her if she would like to go out with him.

It had taken her ten seconds to take in the question, and another fifteen to give him a stammered acceptance, accompanied by a vivid blush. Partially because she was naturally shy, and partially because she had been educated privately at an all girls' school, Genista had had little to do with young men. To her Richard seemed almost godlike. She had heard the village girls chattering about him, and could not understand by what miracle he had actually chosen to ask her out.

The date was for Saturday, four days away, and they passed in a daze of mingled bliss and fear – bliss because Richard had actually asked her out, and fear in case he found her ridiculously childish and lacking in the sophistication he would naturally expect in his dates.

The money she had been carefully hoarding from her salary was withdrawn from her bank account and splurged on a new and – to her – slightly daring outfit which the salesgirl assured her was the very latest fashion – and some new make-up.

Her parents knew about the date, and had been tenderly amused by its effect on her.

Richard was picking her up in his car. It had been a twenty-first present from his father before the latter's death, and Genista was breathless with excitement when she eventually heard it draw up outside the house.

Having promised her parents that he would take the greatest care of her, Richard handed her into the bright red sports car, and that had been the beginning of their romance.

After her initial shyness had gone, Genista had never for one moment doubted that her love for him was returned. Otherwise why would he continue to date her? It was true he never took her to meet his family, nor to the many social gatherings amongst the local farming community to which she knew he was invited, but she believed this was because he wanted them to be alone. Their kisses had gone from shy, tentative embraces to a passionate intensity which left her shaken with a longing she could barely understand. The one occasion upon which Richard touched her breast had filled her with mingled excitement and shame. They had been going out together for six months when Christmas loomed. Richard had already told her that he loved her – and desired her. There was nothing to feel ashamed of, he told her – nor to fear either. He would teach her everything.

Her parents went away the weekend before Christmas. Her father had an important business meeting in London, and her mother was going with him. Genista felt a little nervous about staying in the house alone, but her parents had not suggested that she went with them, and besides, if she had done so, she would have had to miss her weekend date with Richard.

It had been nearly a fortnight since she had seen him. Farm work had kept him busy, he told her vaguely when he picked her up. She had left the house lights on, a little frightened of coming back to an empty house, and they glowed in the darkness as she stepped into the car.

Richard took her to see a film. It remained a dim memory in her mind – men fighting, blood everywhere, women screaming. Afterwards they had driven home slowly, her head on Richard's shoulder. He stopped outside her house, turning her to him and kissing her with a hunger that alarmed and excited her.

Greatly daring, she had asked him in for coffee. It was only when she brought the tray in to the lounge from the kitchen that Richard realised they were alone in the house. His manner had altered subtly, but she had been too naïve to be aware of it. When he took her in his arms, she had responded with all the yearning love locked up in her young heart, barely protesting when his hand slid up under her sweater towards the tender peak of her breast. Her heart was beating so loudly she thought she would suffocate with excitement. Richard was pressing hot, urgent kisses on her face and neck, and through the spiralling excitement she heard him ask why they didn't go upstairs.

The question shocked her. They couldn't, she told him uncertainly. It would be wrong.

Nonsense, he had argued. They loved one another, didn't they?

Genista was quick to agree, adding rather shyly that she had always hoped to be married in white, and that surely it wouldn't be long before they could be married. After all, he had a home to take her to and . . .

In her innocence she was unaware of the reason for his abrupt withdrawal; the angry look on his face as he got up and walked across to the fire, all at once a slightly distant stranger.

'What's the matter?' She had asked the question hesitantly, alarmed by the look in his eyes.

'I can't marry you,' Richard had told her uncompromisingly. 'Where the devil did you get that idea from? I never said anything about marriage.'

'You said you loved me!' It was the cry of a wounded animal caught in a vicious trap, but Richard brushed her words aside, his expression truculent.

'Oh, come on,' he demanded, 'don't give me all that innocent stuff. You knew the score. A passionate little thing like you isn't meant for marriage,' he told her. 'We could have a good time together, Gen.' His confidence was returning and he came and sat down next to her, hugging her against him and trying to kiss her, but Genista moved away. He didn't want to marry her; probably didn't even love her. Inside she was screaming with the agony of it, but outwardly she was as cold as marble.

'I thought you loved me.' At last the words were forced past her numbed lips. 'I thought you wanted to marry me.'

'Marry you?' Her refusal to play the part he had cast for her obviously angered Richard. 'God, my mother would have a fit! I'm going to marry Sir Peter Lawtry's daughter – or so she hopes – not the illegitimate offspring of some small-town solicitor. Marry you? My mother would rather see me dead!'

They must have said other things, but Genista could not remember them. All she could remember was her mingled pain and disbelief, firstly that Richard did not love her, and had merely been using her, while cold-bloodedly contemplating a far more socially advantageous marriage, and secondly that she was, as he had said – illegitimate!

When he finally realised that he was not going to persuade her to go to bed with him either now or ever he had stormed out of the house, calling her such vile names that she felt physically sick with them, and making it plain that he could never have really cared about her. Her dreams in ruins at her feet, Genista had the rest of the weekend to dwell on what he had said before she was able to tackle her parents on their return.

Among the snippets of information Richard had flung at her had been one to the effect that her father had been married to a friend of his mother's before he met Genista's mother. His wife had been tied to a wheelchair following a hunting accident, and although Genista's mother had borne him a child, he had not been free to marry her until after his first wife's death.

Genista tackled her parents the moment they returned home.

They had not denied it. Her mother's eyes had been full of understanding pity as she looked into Genista's white face still haunted by the memory of what Richard had told her.

'In essence everything Richard told you is true, Genista,' she had said later, coming upstairs to where Genista had flung herself down on her bed, trying to come to terms with the truth. 'But try to understand. Your father and I fell very deeply in love. He tried to do the right thing, to send me away, but I wouldn't be sent. You see, I knew he needed me,' she said simply. 'Anne's accident didn't merely rob her of her freedom physically, it also damaged her brain. She was like a child, and your father wouldn't be the man he is if he'd been able to desert her. I respected his decision to stay with her, but he couldn't persuade me to go away and make a new life for myself. He was my life. When I knew I was carrying you I was so pleased. You were the living proof of our love, and I felt no shame. We knew Anne didn't have long to live, and when we were eventually able to marry our happiness was complete, and we've enjoyed it all the more for not having taken it at Anne's expense.'

'But what about me?' Genista cried in anguish. 'I'm illegitimate! Richard's mother would rather die than see him married to me. All he wanted was an affair – he told me so – he said he thought it would be like mother, like daughter.'

Her mother's hand stiffened on the counterpane and then her arms went round Genista's shuddering frame.

'Oh, my poor little girl,' she said softly. 'He's hurt you so badly. You're so very young. I know you won't believe me, but if Richard had really cared about you, nothing his mother might have to say could have prevented him from marrying you. One day you'll meet a man who'll love you, Genista, and he won't care whether your parents were married or not; all he will care about is you.'

The music signalling the end of the programme brought Genista abruptly back to the present. Her mother had been right about Richard not loving her, and since coming to London she had discovered that parentage was of little importance.

The people she worked with accepted her for what she was; and besides, these days illegitimacy meant nothing, but the pain of Richard's betrayal had gone deep and festered. There had been no serious boy-friends in her life since. For a while she had even felt as though she hated her parents, especially when she heard the news of Richard's engagement. Four months later Genista's mother and father were dead. Genista had never ceased to be grateful for the fact that before her parents had left on holiday she had told them that she had come to realise that had Richard genuinely cared for her he would not have been concerned about her birth. She would have hated them to die thinking she blamed them for his defection.

It was high time she put the past behind her, she told herself, but this was easier said than done, especially with men like Luke Ferguson around. A shadow crossed her eyes as she got up to switch the television off. The whole thing had gone beyond a joke. She ought to have made it plain just how wrong his thinking was! Bob's mistress indeed! She wouldn't dwell on his other insults about her mercenary nature. If it wasn't for the fact that it wouldn't be fair to leave Bob in the lurch when he had so many problems on his hands, her notice would be on Luke Ferguson's desk to-morrow morning! She had been horrified to learn from Bob that Luke intended to spend several weeks with them satisfying himself that the company was operating at optimum efficiency. All she could hope for now was that Elaine's doctor would confirm that her tumour was benign, and that she could leave the company without feeling that she was deserting Bob in a time of crisis.

Her hopes were dashed the following morning when she arrived to find Bob already at his desk, wearing a very haggard expression. He greeted her thankfully, pushing a tired hand through hair which seemed to have gone greyer almost overnight.

'Elaine?' Genista asked him sympathetically, eyeing the two empty coffee cups already on his desk. To judge by the amount of paperwork lying there Bob had been in the office for quite some time.

'Bad news, I'm afraid,' Bob told her quietly. 'Our own G.P. came round last night to break the news. I had to take Elaine to the hospital this morning, and they're operating this afternoon. She was so calm,' he told her worriedly, 'too calm, and our doctor agreed with me. It's as though she refuses to accept what's happening. I've tried to talk to her, but she refuses to listen. I'm desperately afraid of what the truth will do to her.'

'You can't shield her from it, Bob,' Genista told him gently. She was about to ask him what time Elaine was having her operation and suggest that he returned to the hospital leaving her to cope with their work, when she became aware that Luke had walked in, and was very obviously eavesdropping on their conversation. His expression was hard to read.

'Bob, can you spare me Genista for the day?' he asked crisply. 'I want to take over the Mellington account myself. They seem to be experiencing problems, and I see that you and Genista both went to see them when they originally requested our services.'

'Mellington?'

Poor Bob, Genista thought sympathetically. He

was obviously far too concerned about Elaine to place the name, but she remembered it—a small firm in Cumbria who specialised in beautiful reproduction furniture. She was not surprised they were having problems. The firm was run by two generations of the family who had founded it, and father and son did not entirely see eye to eye. It had been the son who had wanted to use their services while his father had stubbornly wanted to cling to the old-fashioned methods he had used all his life.

'You remember,' Genista told him, 'that firm up in the Lake District. We went up to see them and spent the weekend there.'

She made the comment in all innocence, forgetting what construction Luke was likely to place upon it. Elaine had gone with them, and Genista had spent most of the weekend alone, exploring the beautiful countryside, leaving Elaine and Bob to enjoy themselves together.

'Oh, good heavens—of course I remember now,' Bob agreed, harassment giving way to pleasure. 'We stayed in that old coaching inn. Our bedroom had a huge fourposter.'

'There isn't time to get there and back in a day,' Genista told Luke, hoping he would change his mind about visiting the factory, but instead a cool gleam entered his eyes, his expression distinctly mocking as he said softly, 'Well, then, we'll just have to stay over, won't we? I shall need one of you with me as you set up the original package, and with Brian still in Amsterdam, I don't think it would be a good idea to take Bob away from the office as well.'

It was on the tip of Genista's tongue to refuse, to tell him that there was no way she was going anywhere with him, but then she looked at Bob, and remembered Elaine. If she refused, Bob would either have to go himself or brief someone to take her place; he had enough on his plate without having to worry about that.

'When were you thinking of going?' she asked Luke, her chin lifting defiantly.

'Today. I'll give you an hour to collect whatever you need, and then I'll pick you up and we can be on our way. Give Jilly the name of the hotel where you stayed, and she can fix us up with rooms.'

'I can drive myself there.' Genista said stiffly. 'There's no need . . .'

Luke's eyebrows rose quellingly.

'And use two separate cars, charging both lots of petrol to expenses? No way. We're travelling together.' He glanced at his watch, flicking back the cuff of an immaculately tailored dark blue suit to reveal the gold wristband strapped to one sinewy wrist. 'Ten minutes of your hour have already gone, and I want to be up there before it gets dark. Our meeting is fixed for tomorrow morning.'

The thought of spending a night under the same roof as Luke Ferguson sent shivers of fear down her spine, but there was no way she could get out of going without adding to Bob's problems, so she swallowed the hot words of refusal clamouring for utterance and went across to Bob, touching him lightly on the shoulder. She knew that Luke was watching them, and she deliberately turned her back to him so that he wouldn't see what she was saying.

'I hope everything goes all right with the op.'

'It's afterwards that I'm worried about,' Bob confided. 'Elaine's always been very insecure, and with this bee she's got in her bonnet just recently about not being attractive any longer. I just don't know how I'm going to reassure her. Still, that's not your problem. Are you sure you don't mind going with Luke, Genista?' he asked awkwardly. 'I know it's none of my business, but I'm very fond of you, and Luke has something of a reputation.'

Genista had to stifle hysterical laughter. Bob warning her about Luke! If only he knew!

She was so determined not to give Luke the opportunity of coming up to her apartment that she packed in record time, pulling clothes haphazardly out of her wardrobe and pushing them into her case, one ear alert for the sound of the intercom warning her that he had arrived. She wouldn't need very much, after all. Clean underwear; an outfit suitable for a business meeting; her jeans just in case she managed to get any free time, and something comfortable to travel in.

She was just snapping her case together and tying the buckles when the intercom buzzed.

'I'm on my way,' she told George, hoping to forestall any attempt on Luke's part to come upstairs, but to her dismay it was his darkly velvet tones she heard floating into the room, as he told her he was on his way up.

Feeling flustered, she pulled on the jacket of the suede suit she had decided to wear for travelling, snatching up her handbag and pausing uncertainly in the middle of her elegant living room while she waited for the bell to ring. Even so, when it did so the sound sent fear spiralling along her nerves. Her fingers trembled as she unlocked the door. She had meant to keep Luke standing in the small hall while she got her case, but he followed her into the living room, looking round appreciatively.

'Very pleasant,' he said at last. 'Bob must think an awful lot of you.'

His cynical tone jarred, and Genista paused on the threshold to her bedroom, her fingers tightly gripped round the handle of her case, unaware of how vividly beautiful she appeared, framed there, her russet hair set off by the soft moss green suede suit, her eyes glowing brilliantly with the emotions she was fighting hard to control.

'Just as I think a good deal of him,' she said quietly.

'Do you?' There was disbelief in the words, and something else she could not put a name to. The colour seemed to have left Luke's face. His eyes were hard, almost completely black; obsidian, she thought absently, cold and unfeeling.

'So much so that you want to break up his marriage?'

'I don't want to break it up.' The words were out before she could stop them, her face drained of colour.

'Prove it,' Luke said quietly. 'Marry me.'

'Marry you?' Her voice sounded weak and husky, her eyes mirroring the shock his words had given her. 'You don't mean that. You . . .'

'I wouldn't say it if I didn't mean it. Marry me, Genista, otherwise I'll make sure Bob's wife gets to hear about your affair.'

'You'd do that? But why?'

She was genuinely puzzled. She could understand that he might try to use such a threat to force her to sleep with him, but marriage? He couldn't possibly want to marry her; he had made his contempt of her all too plain.

'Why?' There was a tortured expression in his eyes, a look of self-loathing which shocked her with its intensity.

'Because since I met you I haven't slept or eaten;

because something about you torments me night and day. I must possess you, Genista. It's like a sickness that won't let me go.'

'But marriage!'

'I don't want to have to share you with anyone else,' he told her grimly, 'or to be dangled on the end of a piece of string to flatter your vanity. Oh, it won't last. One day I'll wake up and find I'm free of this obsession which seems to haunt me, and then I'll divorce you, but until then you'll be my possession, to do with as I please.'

'And if I refuse to marry you?' Genista asked. Her throat was dry with tension. An obsession he had called his desire to possess her, and that was what it was; a hunger fuelled by her own foolish attempt to humiliate him. For a moment it crossed her mind that she might be wiser simply to open the door and run, but common sense reminded her that she wouldn't be allowed to get very far. But marriage!

'If you refuse I shall make sure Elaine knows all about your affair; about this apartment; about the weekend you and Bob spent together; the car he bought you . . .'

'It's not true!' Genista told him angrily. 'None of it's true. We aren't having an affair; I own this apartment in my own right. Bob is a very good friend . . .'

'And you care enough about him to want to protect him. I didn't think you had it in you, but it won't work. I meant every word I said, Genista. It's either marriage to me, or I tell Elaine everything.'

In normal circumstances Genista would not have hesitated. She would have gone straight to Bob and warned him so that he could tell Elaine, but

Elaine's operation and state of mind meant that this was impossible. If Luke told Elaine now that she and Bob were having an affair, she was only too likely to believe it. For one mad moment Genista contemplated going to see Elaine herself, but then acknowledged that this would probably only serve to make them appear more guilty. Luke definitely had the upper hand, she thought bitterly, but marriage——!

'Why marriage?' she demanded again. 'Why not a brief affair? A one-night stand, even? After all, that's all I'm fit for, according to you, isn't it?'

Dark colour ran up under his skin as she flung the words at him. He came to stand over her, his fingers biting into the soft flesh of her upper arms, his eyes burning so hotly that she wondered how she could ever have thought of them as cold.

'I've told you why. I can't analyse my need for you, Genista. It defies all the laws of logic. I know you're a cheap little tramp who sells her favours in return for financial gain; I know you don't give a damn who you hurt or how, but God help me, I still want you so badly it's like an ache in the gut, and it won't be assuaged simply by one act of possession. You might as well offer a starving man a crumb of bread!'

His words frightened her; showing her the intensity of his desire for her. It was like a sickness, she thought, shivering under the look in his eyes. Richard too had wanted her, and had been prepared to lie to her by pretending love for her to satisfy what was merely sexual need, but Luke was prepared to go to even further lengths.

'I want your decision now,' he told her harshly, cutting across her thoughts. 'Either we return from this trip as man and wife, or I tell Elaine all about your relationship with her husband.'

He really meant it, Genista acknowledged. Her heart felt as though it were being squeezed by giant hands, her breathing shallow and uneven as she contemplated the prospect of being Luke's wife. A shudder ran through her as she remembered that soul-destroying kiss he had forced upon her. And that had only been a kiss! Even now she could remember how it had besmirched her, making her feel as cheap as the sort of woman he accused her of being.

'If I agree, I'll lose Bob anyway,' she realised, desperately trying to find a loophole for herself. Instinct told her that there was no point in trying to plead with him by revealing Elaine's dangerous emotional state; he would merely use the information as an additional lever.

'You're damned right you will!' Luke swore savagely. 'I don't intend to share you with anyone else, Genista, but this way at least you keep your pride. He won't leave Elaine for you, you must know that, and if you do care about him you won't want to try and break up a marriage that obviously means a good deal to him. Strange, I shouldn't have thought you the type of woman who shares her man. Or as long as he keeps on paying the bills, don't you care?'

Genista longed to scream at him that he was completely wrong. She paid her own bills, and cared for Bob only as a friend, but she knew he would not believe her. He was so biased against her, so convinced that he was right that nothing would change his mind. While she stared sightlessly across the room he walked past her and into her bedroom, strolling casually round it, while the words of bitter fury froze on her lips.

'Odd,' he mused, glancing at the delicate feminine room with its pale peach decor. 'It doesn't
give the impression of a room that's shared by a
man and woman.' Before she could stop him, he
opened a wardrobe door, studying the clothes
hanging there.

'Nice,' he commented, 'and expensive. Where
does Bob keep his things? Or is he too discreet to
leave any of the evidence lying about?'

Feeling too sick to reply, Genista walked towards the kitchen. Perhaps a glass of water could
clear the nausea rising in her throat. She was
reaching for a glass when she heard Luke behind
her, his tall, lean frame filling the small room.

'Well?' he enquired grimly. 'What's the answer?'

'If I had only myself to consider there is just no
way I would agree,' she told him in a shaky voice.
'What you're doing is blackmail—there's no other
way to describe it. The thought of making love
with you makes me feel ill!' Her voice started to
rise hysterically on the last few words, and she
gasped as hard fingers dug into her shoulders,
turning her painfully so that she was facing Luke,
the broad expanse of his white shirt blurring a little
as tears filled her eyes.

'Does it now?' he grated in a voice laced with
threatening menace. 'Well, we'll just have to see if
we can't change your mind about that, won't we?
Not now,' he told her, as the colour left her face,
leaving her vulnerable to the knowing probe of his
dark eyes. 'When I take you, Genista, I want to
savour the experience, not rush through it like a
callow adolescent. And you will savour it,' he told
her softly, the pressure of his fingers no longer
painful, but persuasive, as they lingered on the frail
bones of her shoulders, impelling her forward until

her breasts were touching the dark wool of his jacket. 'I'll make you respond to me,' he murmured against her hair. 'Whatever pleasure Bob gave you, I'll give you more.'

'You couldn't!' The words were torn from her throat in a terrified cry. For a moment his words had almost mesmerised her; her heart was pounding unsteadily, sensations that turned her cold with fear, curling insidiously through her stomach, weakening her legs to the point where she wanted only to lean against Luke's lean body. Her emotions shocked and terrified her. She hated the man, and yet just for a moment the images conjured up by his soft words had weakened her defences to the point where she had actually experienced a sharp stab of physical desire!

'Try me.'

The sexually explicit invitation left her feeling nervously frightened. They were, after all, completely alone in the flat. She moistened her lips, unaware of the teasing provocation of the movement until she glanced up and saw the raw hunger burning in Luke's eyes.

'Don't tempt me,' he advised her harshly. 'Now, do I tell Elaine about you and Bob, or are you going to marry me?'

Did she really have any choice? Dared she risk Elaine's health and possibly her marriage by refusing? But if she married Luke, ultimately he would discover that he had been wrong. A hot flush of colour surged over her body as she dwelt on exactly how he would discover the truth, and she started to tremble violently at the thought of the intimacies marriage would entitle him to. Perhaps she could agree, and then find some means of escaping. If she could just get him out of the flat; just persuade him to wait until Elaine was over the operation.

'I'm not going to wait, Genista,' he told her, as though he had the power to follow her thoughts. 'And don't try running out on me. If you do I shall tell Elaine. I want your answer now.'

Genista took a deep breath. For Bob's sake she had to do it.

Marriages could be annulled. She could find some way of keeping Luke at bay until Elaine was better.

'Very well, I'll marry you.' Her lips felt swollen and dry and she badly wanted to lick them again, but fear of what the gesture might provoke prevented her.

'Very wise,' Luke said softly. 'But don't start thinking about a long engagement. We're getting married today.'

'Today?' Her heart came into her mouth. 'But . . . but that's impossible!'

'Not with an archbishop's licence and an archdeacon for an uncle,' Luke told her drily. He pushed back his cuff in a gesture which was becoming familiar to her. The sight of the dark hairs curling crisply against the gold strap of his watch made her stomach knot with apprehension. Some instinct told her that his body would be totally masculine, and her fingers curled moistly into the palms of her hands as she contemplated its enforced possession of her.

'It will take me about an hour to make the arrangements. We can be married in Cumbria. And don't even think about running out on me, because if you do I'll find you, and I'll make sure Elaine knows exactly what's been going on between you and her husband. While I'm gone I suggest you occupy your time in finding something suitable to be married in.' He pulled out his wallet and wrote a cheque, signing it firmly, and tossing it across to her. 'On second thoughts, go out and buy yourself something, I won't have my bride wearing clothes paid for by another man.'

'And I won't wear anything bought with your money!' Genista flung back at him. 'I'd rather be stark naked!'

'An enticing prospect,' Luke drawled coolly, 'but I have a rather old-fashioned urge to be the only one to see my bride's nudity. And don't tear that cheque up, because if you do, I'll take you out and buy you something myself.'

'I'm surprised you don't anyway,' Genista raged, goaded beyond endurance. 'What am I supposed to buy? Something white? If I had my way I'd be wearing mourning!'

For a moment there was a flicker of some emotion she could not name in the depths of the charcoal grey eyes, but then it was gone, his mouth uncompromisingly firm as he looked her up and down.

'Save the amateur dramatics for those who appreciate them,' he advised her dryly. 'A simple suit should suffice. Whatever else you might lack, no one could accuse you of not having taste. Just remember that we shall be getting married in a small country church and that no one apart from ourselves will know that it isn't a perfectly normal marriage.'

'When in reality it's merely a legal vehicle for you to satisfy your libido,' Genista said bitterly. 'And once you have, I'm to be flung aside like so much unwanted trash.'

'I couldn't have put it better myself,' Luke said smoothly. 'One hour, Genista—and remember, if

you're not here, I go straight to Elaine and tell her
about your affair with her husband.'

When he had gone Genista sank down into the
nearest chair, her legs trembling with fear and
reaction.

Marriage to Luke Ferguson! Even now she
could not believe it was actually going to happen;
that the whole thing wasn't merely some terrible
nightmare. It was all real enough, she told herself
soberly, her eyes alighting on the phone. A last
desperate hope came to her, and she picked up the
receiver, dialling the office number, and asking for
Bob.

'He's at the hospital,' Jilly told her. 'They called
him—something about Elaine. Apparently she
needs a fairly major operation. I've never seen him
look so worried. Can I take a message for him?'

After telling Jilly that it wasn't anything important, Genista hung up slowly. She felt like an animal
driven far below the earth, its every avenue of
escape slowly blocked off. The chiming of the old
grandfather clock which had belonged to her
parents reminded her that she had barely forty-five
minutes of her hour left. She glanced distastefully
at Luke's cheque, still reluctant to use it, and then
she remembered a suit she had bought the previous
month. It was still hanging in her wardrobe as yet
unworn. She had bought it for the christening of a
friend's baby. It was in a very soft shade of pale
green; a three-piece comprising a skirt in silk chiffon, slenderly fitting and finely pleated at the back;
a pretty camisole top, and a long-sleeved jacket
which gave the outfit a more formal air. Without it
the camisole and skirt could easily pass for a dress,
and there was even a hat in matching chiffon
trimmed with soft pink roses. Genista remembered

that when she had been trying it on the salesgirl had commented that it would be ideal for a summer wedding. Genista had agreed, never for one moment dreaming that she would be wearing it for her own. It had been many years since she thought about getting married—since Richard, in fact, but that did not alter the fact that had she so desired she had every right to be married in a misty froth of white with all the traditional trimmings.

The case she had packed earlier was in the living room, and she refused to add anything else to it. This was no true marriage; she had no need of a normal bride's fripperies. The first thing she saw when she opened the case to pack the silk suit was the Oriental housecoat she had placed on top of her other clothes, and she averted her eyes from the rich jade silk. She had bought it in Hong Kong and loved the feel of the fabric next to her skin. It was designed on the lines of a cheongsam and she knew that it suited the slender lines of her body. No man had ever seen her wearing it, and none would, she told herself fiercely. She would find some way of preventing Luke from consummating this parody of a marriage.

She had just closed the case when Luke returned. He had changed out of the suit he had been wearing earlier and was dressed in hip-hugging jeans and a thin knit shirt which clung to the sleek muscles of his back and chest. The shirt was open at the neck, and Genista felt the familiar fear curl through her stomach as she saw the dark hair shadowing his chest.

'Ready?'

How could he sound so cool? The man who had told her that it was his desire for her that was forcing him into this marriage seemed to have completely disappeared, to be replaced by this cool, distant, arrogantly male creature, whose presence in her home intimidated and alarmed her.

'I've made all the arrangements. We'll be married in Cumbria, spend the weekend there and then return to London.'

Not a word about where they were to live; what she was supposed to do about her job or what his family thought about his sudden decision to marry—and to a girl they had never seen, Genista thought incredulously, watching him lift her case as though it weighed no more than a handbag.

'What are you waiting for?'

His sardonic words jerked her to her feet, and like someone in a dream she followed him out of the apartment.

CHAPTER FOUR

MOTORWAYS provide a fast but very monotonous means of traversing the country, Genista thought, watching the landscape flash past as the Maserati ate up the miles. Lancaster had come and gone; the scenery grew gradually wilder. The empty feeling in the pit of her stomach reminded her that it was past her normal lunchtime. She snatched a brief look at Luke's remote profile. He had not talked to her at all during their drive, and she had been quite happy to let him concentrate on the motorway, even though her thoughts were not happy ones. He had arranged a special licence, he had told her before they left London, and his uncle had made all the arrangements with the small church where they were to be married.

'My parents were married there,' Luke had told her, and the brief comment had aroused her curiosity.

The Maserati slowed down, and Genista glanced at Luke again. 'I thought we'd stop for lunch. There's an excellent hotel not far from here. We used to eat there whenever we travelled north.'

'Do your parents live in Cumbria?' Genista probed, curious to learn a little more of his background. If they did, it was not inconceivable that she might meet them, and they could prove to be allies.

'No,' Luke said shortly, quenching her hopes. 'They're dead—they were killed in a road accident several years ago. Now there's just my sister and myself. Marina is divorced. She lives in France with her daughter. Her husband left her for his secretary.' His mouth twisted. 'A story with which I'm sure you're quite familiar. Unfortunately Marina was very sheltered by our parents. She's never really got over the blow, and Lucy is left to run wild when she isn't at school, while Marina broods.'

'I'm sorry.' The trite words were low, but she meant them. She was surprised that Luke had told her so much, but then of course he could hardly keep their marriage a secret, and she would be expected to know something about his background.

'Your parents are dead too, of course.' He shot a sideways glance, perceiving her sudden start of surprise. 'It was on your staff records.'

'Oh?' Something in the way his eyes slid over her, assessing the shape of her body beneath her clothes, provoked her into saying bitterly, 'Did they also tell you that I'm illegitimate? That my mother bore me without benefit of marriage? That my father was married at the time but gave her a child anyway?'

'It happens.'

His laconic response halted her. She half turned in her seat as they left the motorway, her forehead furrowed. 'Aren't you shocked? Aren't you going to say like mother, like daughter?'

'Ought I to? I've never been able to understand why our society casts the slur of illegitimacy on innocent children. They're not to blame for their parents' actions. A true case of the sins of the fathers, I suppose. Is that what made you the way you are?' he demanded, catching her off guard. 'A deep-seated desire to get back at all men for the fact that your father caused you to be illegitimate?'

'No,' Genista told him shortly. 'My parents loved one another very deeply. For a time I did resent what had happened, but I didn't know until I was in my teens, so I was spared a lot of the agony.'

'And suffered a great deal more when you eventually discovered the truth,' Luke hazarded shrewdly. 'Who told you? An interfering gossip?'

'No. The man I thought loved me,' Genista heard herself saying to her horror. 'Only of course he didn't. How could he love me? I was illegitimate, unworthy. No, all he wanted was to sleep with me.'

She was unaware of the bitterness in her voice; tears forming in her eyes, which she blinked quickly away. It would never do to break down in front of Luke!

'And did he?'

The question puzzled her. She looked up, the

muscles of her throat tightening as she saw the look
in his eyes.

'Did he sleep with you, Genista?' he pressed.

There was no way she could tell him the truth.
She had told him too much already—things she
had told no one else; secrets she had kept close to
her heart all her life.

'What do you think?'

A muscle jerked in his jaw, his hands tightening
on the steering wheel until the knuckles gleamed
whitely through the tanned skin.

'You were a fool,' he told her harshly. 'You
should have refused him.'

'Why? So that you could be first?' She could have
bitten her tongue out the moment the words were
uttered. She had no idea what had prompted her
to utter them. Luke's expression was savagely
angry, and she was glad that the narrow road
demanded his concentration. He looked as though
he would have liked to strangle her, but she had
no idea why. 'I thought men didn't go for virgins
these days,' she added, trying to make the words
sound light. 'Experience is all the vogue.'

'You're right, of course.' Luke's voice was completely impersonal. 'Inexperience causes fear, which
in turn lessens both parties' pleasure.' He shrugged,
and Genista saw the powerful muscles beneath his
shirt contract and expand. 'Virginity in itself is
nothing, but I suspect deep inside every man lurks
the desire to teach the woman he loves to respond
to him, and him alone.'

His words touched a chord deep inside her she
had never known she possessed, causing her an
aching pain which seemed to spread endlessly
through her body in waves of anguish, and yet why,
she did not know. She did not love Luke and he

did not love her. But he would be the first man to make love to her, stealing from a man who might love her the right to teach her. She shrugged the thought away. She had never intended to marry, never believed in love, so what did it matter? This marriage was something that must be endured for Bob's sake. A sudden thought struck her. Surely if he found her cold and unresponsive Luke would soon lose his desire for her, and wish their marriage over? And she wouldn't need to act the part. Already she was dreading being alone with him, her body rigid with terror at the thought of having him touch her.

'Hungry?'

She had been totally engrossed in her thoughts and realised that the Maserati had come to rest in the forecourt of a large Victorian hotel. She wasn't really hungry, but it was obvious that Luke intended them to eat, and as she was fast beginning to learn, he wasn't a man one could argue with and win.

His courtesy as he helped her out of the car was something which surprised her, until she reminded herself that his excellent manners were probably an automatic reflex of which he was possibly unaware. The hotel was imposing, the red brick façade faintly awe-inspiring. A flight of shallow stone steps led upwards to the entrance, and as they stepped into the cool tiled foyer. Genista looked around the elegant high-ceilinged room appreciatively.

'It was originally a country house,' Luke told her informatively. 'The scene of many a weekend party, or so I should imagine, but after the war it was turned into a hotel.'

The head waiter materialised in front of them,

and obviously recognised Luke. They were shown
to a small table overlooking the gardens with a
deference that Genista found enlightening. She had
thought of Luke only in context with herself, and
now it was brought home to her that she was
marrying a very important man; and certainly an
exceedingly wealthy one.

She was handed a menu which she studied
absently.

'If you're not feeling particularly hungry, I
suggest you start with the river trout,' Luke said
quietly. 'They're a speciality of the hotel.'

Genista did as he suggested, and as he had
promised the fish was delicious. She had ordered
fillet steak for her main meal with a side salad, and
although the steak was beautifully tender she was
unable to eat more than a couple of mouthfuls.
Seated opposite Luke in the elegant surroundings
of the restaurant with its thick pile carpet and glid-
ing waiters, she felt the enormity of her situation
suddenly come home to her. She all but choked on
her steak, pushing her plate away, as she stared
blindly into space. What had she agreed to? She
wouldn't marry Luke. She couldn't marry him! She
stole a glance at his imperious profile. He appeared
absorbed in his food. Her eyes rested on the strong
male features of his face, trying to relax her taut
nerves. Luke beckoned the wine waiter and
murmured something to him, and for a moment
the man's impassive features relaxed into a smile.
He disappeared, returning several minutes later
with an ice bucket containing a green bottle, and
two champagne glasses.

'Drink it,' Luke commanded when the frothing
liquid had been poured. 'It will help calm your
nerves.'

'So would a cup of Horlicks,' Genista murmured irreverently. It seemed wrong to be drinking champagne—a drink she had always associated with happy celebrations—before this forced wedding.

'Horlicks is a bedtime drink,' Luke said softly. 'Do you have trouble getting to sleep, Genista? I'm not surprised, with all that you must have on your conscience. They do say that healthy exercise is an excellent cure.'

Her cheeks burned, as much at the implication of his last words as at the earlier insult. Tears burned against the back of her throat, and all at once she felt unable to fight any longer. A terrible feeling of misery engulfed her, a lassitude so foreign to her nature that she couldn't understand why she should be experiencing it. It was as though her mind was at last acknowledging that there was nothing more she could do to escape and it was trying to teach her body acceptance.

Luke had ordered strawberries and fresh cream for dessert. He himself had cheese and biscuits, and Genista pushed the fruit round her dish, until his muttered exasperation got through to her.

'I don't want it,' she told him defiantly. 'All I want is for everything to be over . . .'

'And for things to be as they were before,' Luke finished for her.

Self-pity welled up inside her.

'Things can never be as they were,' she told him fiercely, flinching a little at the inimical look in his eyes as they searched her flushed face.

'No, they can't, can they?' he agreed softly. 'And I warn you now, Genista, if I think for one moment that you're thinking of Bob when I make love to you, I'll make you sorry you were ever born.'

'You already have,' Genista said recklessly. 'And

you can't tell me what to think, Luke. My thoughts
at least are still my own.'

She could feel the anger beating up inside him,
and wondered shiveringly what would happen if
he ever unleashed it. She hoped she never got to
find out.

It was two o'clock when they left the hotel. They
didn't return to the motorway, but drove through
the dales, lonely, magnificent country dotted with
sheep, and laced with ancient grey stone walls.
Villages huddled in the valleys, single streets of tiny
cottages by rivers, so clean and clear that Genista
could see the river bed as they drove past. The sun
shone sporadically, casting shadows which chased
each other over the rolling hills as clouds drifted
over the sun. In other circumstances the peace of
her surroundings must surely have had a relaxing
effect upon her, she reflected, but today she was
too tense, too highly strung to appreciate the time-
less beauty of the countryside.

Kendal, with its limestone walls and houses, was
busy. They drove straight through, Luke concentrating on his driving. In Windermere she gazed at
the blue-grey expanse of the lake, her tension tightening into coils of fear that slid agonisingly through
her stomach. The road circled the lake before
climbing steeply into hills so old and weathered by
time that Genista caught her breath in awe.

The road seemed to wind for an eternity through
woods which she suspected must be heartbreak-
ingly lovely in the autumn before emerging
among the hills. The faint baaing of the sheep
was the only sound to disturb the stillness of the
afternoon. High above in the sky Genista saw a
bird hovering motionless.

'A peregrine falcon,' Luke told her, following her

gaze. 'There's a place up here where they train them. There's a huge export demand for the birds, especially in the Middle East. I suppose there's something of the pagan in all men which responds to the ultimate primitive thrill of taming so much splendour.'

The knot of fear in Genista's stomach tightened. It wasn't hard to imagine one of those proud birds, wings outstretched, fierce claws digging into a leatherbound wrist as Luke fed it raw meat. There was something primitive about him, she thought uneasily; something that refused to be tamed by civilisation. The knowledge unnerved her, and if they hadn't been on such a deserted stretch of road she might have contemplated trying to escape.

The road dipped suddenly. Below them she could see a small village, the church spire reaching up towards the clouds.

Half a dozen children were playing in the village square, and they scattered when Luke stopped the car, gazing at it with open-mouthed awe.

Despite the fact that the afternoon was mild, Genista felt goosebumps rise up under her skin as Luke helped her out of the car. In silence he led the way to the small vicarage set next to the church.

'The Vicar here was a close friend of my parents,' he told her quietly as he opened the garden gate. 'One wrong word, one glance to show that this marriage is not desired by both of us, and I'll make tonight something you'll want to blot out of your mind for the rest of your life.'

Genista shivered, pressing her hand to temples which had begun to ache badly. For some reason Luke seemed to sap all her normal resilience. In his presence she felt as capable as a small child faced with a domineering adult. Mindlessly she allowed him to propel her up the garden path. It was bordered by lavender which smelled heavenly, she noticed absently, and old-fashioned pink roses climbed over the Vicarage walls to mingle with the honeysuckle and clematis.

The door opened before they could reach it, and a plump woman with soft brown hair, touched with grey, and a delighted smile hurried towards them. She embraced Luke first, tilting back her head to stare up at him. She barely reached his shoulder, and there were tears in her eyes as she turned from him to Genista.

'Oh, Luke, she's lovely!' she said emotionally. 'When John told me you wanted to be married here, I was so thrilled. Luke's parents were married in this church,' she told Genista. 'But I expect you already know that. But you should have given us more warning, Luke.' Her smile robbed the words of any criticism, and Genista could see that she was very fond of Luke.

'Amy is my godmother,' he explained to Genista as their hostess turned away to open the front door. 'Since the death of my parents she and John are the nearest thing I've had to a family.'

The Vicarage hall was dark after the sunlit garden, and Genista stumbled over the step and would have fallen if Luke's arm hadn't caught her round the waist. Just for a second her body was pressed against the hard warmth of his, and a feeling not unlike panic swept over her. Amy turned, beaming at them both, and her fear subsided a little. Luke was unlikely to do anything to her in someone else's presence.

'Luke told me you both wanted to get changed before the ceremony. Luke's in his usual room, but

I've put you in our daughter's. Where are you taking her for the honeymoon, Luke?' she asked her godson. 'Or is it a secret?'

It was impossible not to like the small, motherly woman. Genista felt drawn to her immediately, and in other circumstances—had she not been so obviously under Luke's spell—she might have risked confiding in her and begging for her help. However, it was simply not possible. It was obvious that she expected Genista to be over the moon with joy at the thought of marrying Luke, and moreover, believed that they were madly in love. Narrow twisting stairs led off the hall, and as she followed her hostess up them Genista heard Luke saying behind her, 'It's a secret, Amy. Unfortunately we've only got a long weekend.'

'You work far too hard,' she reproved him. 'You must make him slow down,' she told Genista. 'A long weekend! You're lucky she agreed to marry you, Luke. I would have insisted on a month— preferably on some gorgeous tropical island.'

'Haven't you noticed? Genista's a redhead. She'd be suffering from sunburn before the first day was out, and that's no good on a honeymoon.'

Amy tried to look disapproving and failed. Genista forced a smile, knowing that something was expected of her. She could have told them both that her skin didn't burn, but she sensed that to do so would bring Luke's anger down upon her hapless head, and she already had enough to cope with without that.

The room Amy showed her to was prettily feminine. Luke brought up her suitcase while Amy was still chatting about his childhood, and how delighted she and her husband were that they'd chosen to be married in his church.

'I've been down this morning and done the flowers. June is such a lovely month for a wedding, but we don't get many here, unfortunately. The young people move away to the towns looking for jobs, and marry there. John's in his study, if you want to have a word with him,' she told Luke as he placed Genista's case on the bed. 'We've arranged the ceremony for four, to give you time to get to wherever it is you're going afterwards.'

'I'll go down and have a word with him after I've showered and changed.'

He went, closing the door behind him, and fresh panic engulfed Genista. She turned blindly towards the window, unaware that Amy had caught a glimpse of her face until the older woman said softly,

'It's such a big step, isn't it? But you couldn't entrust your life to a better man. Luke's parents' marriage was exceptionally happy. His father had old-fashioned values and both Luke and Marina were brought up on them. I think that's why Marina took it so hard when her husband left her. For a while we thought Luke might never marry. It seemed to harden him, and then ... Well, the fact that the girl Philip ran off with was Luke's girl-friend was an added complication. Marina blamed him for introducing Verity to Philip. She couldn't seem to see that Luke had been hurt as well.' Amy sighed. 'Forgive me, my dear, this isn't the time to bring up all that sad business again. I'm so glad Luke's found happiness. He deserves it, and I'm sure you'll make him very happy.' She patted Genista's hand and laughed. 'You probably think we're too old-fashioned to be aware of these things, but I can recognise love when I see it, and love for you is written all over Luke's face.'

Amy was mistaking love for sexual desire, Genista thought wearily as the door closed behind the older woman.

Alone, she showered quickly in the small en-suite bathroom attached to the bedroom, drying herself briskly on one of the large fluffy towels Amy had supplied, before slipping into the silky briefs she had pulled out of her case. Because of the camisole top to the suit it was impossible to wear a bra, but the sheer fabric was lined, and although the soft swell of her breasts was clearly visible beneath the fabric, there was nothing offensive about it. The hem on her skirt brushed her silk stockings, and she slid on fragile leather sandals in a toning shade of green before sitting down to apply her make-up.

Her skin glowed healthily from her holiday and she had no need to use foundation. The merest hint of soft lilac eyeshadow added depth to her amethyst eyes. She brushed her lashes sparingly with mascara, and added soft pink lipstick before brushing her hair until it crackled.

She was just spraying her skin with perfume when she heard the rap on the door, and she opened it nervously, blinking a little in surprise at the strange man standing there.

'I'm Jeff Stanley. Luke asked me to do the honours—I hope you don't mind? We used to play together when we were kids. I'm the local doctor here. My wife and I are going to act as your witnesses, and as Amy flatly refused to allow Luke to see you in your wedding finery, I was deputised to escort you to the church. An honour and a privilege,' he added with an admiring grin. 'Now I've seen you I know why Luke was so reluctant to leave you. I don't suppose he'd appreciate it if I took my best man's kiss in advance!'

He was obviously trying to help her to relax, but Genista felt as stiff as a poker as they walked along the lavender-bordered path to the small, grey country church. In other circumstances the simple service in the plain whitewashed church would have been her ideal. The flowers arranged by Amy made a soft pool of colour against the white background. Light streamed in through the stained glass windows—a gift to the church by a seventeenth-century inhabitant of the village, and obviously cherished.

Amy's husband, John Robson, was as homey and pleasant as his wife. His voice was the one which guided Genista through her responses—responses which were tying her irrevocably to the man at her side, giving him licence to do with her as he wished. At one point she thought her voice was going to desert her completely, and only the hard grip of Luke's fingers round her wrist jerked her back to awareness. And then at last it was over. The church bells pealed, and a small crowd had gathered outside to wish them well, and stare at the bride. Jeff Stanley did kiss her, but only lightly on the cheek before turning her back to Luke with a wide grin.

'She's all yours now, you lucky man. Barbara has prepared a buffet up at the house, but you aren't expected to stay long. We're still able to remember what it feels like to be newly married. I expect you can't wait to be on your own. Aren't you going to kiss the bride?' he added.

Genista shrank back as Luke's arm circled her waist. But it was too late. He was already drawing her towards him, his cool breath fanning the tendrils of hair at her temples, as his dark head bent towards her, blotting out the sun. It was that night

in the alleyway all over again, and she tensed in
fear, panic spreading through her body like fire.
She was trembling so badly that she knew Luke
must have felt it. His lips felt cool as they touched
her own, his eyes night-dark as she looked up into
them, pools of emptiness in which she could drown
if she let herself. His body was shielding her from
the onlookers, and to them they probably looked
much like any other newly married couple, exchanging a brief embrace. Luke's lips didn't linger.
The butterfly embrace was over almost before it
had begun, leaving her feelings vaguely cheated,
although she was at a loss to understand the reason
for this strange emotion.

Jeff Stanley's wife was plump and pretty. They
had been married two years and had a very active
nine-month-old son.

'Luke's a real dreamboat, isn't he?' she commented to Genista when she had taken her upstairs
to show her the baby. 'I used to have the most
dreadful crush on him. How did you meet?'

'At a party,' Genista said truthfully. Even now
she could not believe that they were actually
married.

'Come on down, you two,' Jeff called. 'Luke's
champing at the bit! I'd hurry if I were you,
Genista,' he teased. 'He's not a patient man and I
suspect he's longing to get you to himself.'

Genista hadn't changed out of her suit; there
seemed little point. She had no idea where Luke
was taking her. He had cancelled the business
meeting which had been the original purpose of
their journey, she knew that.

Seated in the car, waiting for Luke to join her,
she felt her stomach tensing nervously. She was on
her honeymoon, the thought brought anxiety

crawling along her nerves. She was just on the point of thrusting open the car door and screaming that she couldn't go through with it, when Luke slid in beside her, turning the key in the ignition.

'Come back soon!' Amy called as the Maserati slid out of the square. 'Have a good time!'

'Where are you taking me?'

She sounded like an abducted heroine, Genista thought crossly. The worst possible thing she could do was to show fear. She ought to be showing Luke that she felt completely in control of the situation. Tonight he fully expected that he would be sharing her bed, but she knew that she could not allow him to do so, and if she panicked she would have next to no chance of preventing him.

'It's a surprise,' was all he would say, but he said it in such a grim tone that Genista felt her nervousness increase. She should never have allowed herself to be manoeuvred into this position. She should have told him right from the start that he was completely wrong about her. A confession trembled on her lips, but she quickly realised that telling him the truth would serve no useful purpose. He would still desire her, perhaps even more when he knew that he would be her first lover. Her pulse rate quickened as she remembered what he had said at her apartment.

'Where are you taking me?' she demanded huskily.

'Frightened?' The mocking question sawed at her raw nerve ends. 'There's no need to be. After all, I won't be the first man to share your bed, but I intend to be the one you remember the longest, Genista.'

'Sure of yourself, aren't you?'

She could feel him watching her, the knowledge

sending prickly warnings along her skin.

'No more than any other man with experience of your sex. The act of love is one which should be mutually enjoyable, and I believe that our body chemistry is such that it will be. You can't deny that you responded to me when I kissed you.'

'I hated it,' Genista interrupted, her voice trembling with the fear the memory aroused. 'And I hate you!'

The scenery had become vaguely familiar, and with a growing sense of disbelief she realised that they were approaching the hotel where she had stayed with Bob and Elaine.

'Recognise it?' Luke asked sardonically. 'I asked Jilly to book us a double room. I got the impression she disapproved. No doubt she'll be extremely relieved to see that on your hand when we return,' he added, lifting Genista's left hand, where her new rings glittered on her finger.

She had been surprised when Luke produced both an engagement and wedding ring. They had obviously been designed to be worn together, the single beautiful diamond of the engagement ring, set into a fine platinum band cut to match the gold and platinum wedding ring.

'Am I allowed to return to the office?' Genista retaliated sarcastically, as much to hide her growing fear as anything else. 'Would you trust me so close to Bob?'

'No, but I trust him,' came Luke's laconic response. 'And you won't be returning to work—just making a visit to let everyone know how the land lies. I don't want Bob accusing me of doing away with you. Once he knows we're married . . .'

'He won't be tempted to resume our affair, is that what you're thinking? What makes you think

I can't make him overcome his scruples? After all,
desire for me led you to overcome yours. I can't
really be the sort of woman you wanted for a wife;
a businessman such as yourself—surely you wanted
a wife you could be proud of, someone who would
play her part as your hostess, impress your business
colleagues.'

'I'm sure you'll be able to do that,' Luke said
dryly. 'And as for the rest, I learned long ago that
a man has to accept women for what they are, not
what he would like them to be.'

'Because of Verity?'

'Who told you about her?' The sharpness of the
question betrayed his anger that she knew about
the other woman.

'Amy let it slip. When you said that your sister
had been deserted by her husband, I didn't realise
that he'd gone off with your girl-friend.'

'Verity was the one who did the "going off",
as you term it. Philip was already a successful
businessman while I was still struggling, and no
doubt Verity thought him the better proposition.
As it turned out she was wrong, but it taught me
a lesson I've never forgotten. You might remember
that if you are tempted to cheat on me, Genista.'

'I wouldn't dream of it.' She said it tauntingly,
but it was true. The more she came to learn about
this man, the more she wondered at her own blind
folly in provoking him in the first place. One look
at him was all it took to realise the steel will
cloaked by the sensual body, but for some reason
she had been completely unaware of the danger
lurking in the depths of the cold grey eyes the first
time they met. Her mind had been on other
things, of course; the takeover of the company, but
that did not totally excuse her. It was too late to

regret her shortsightedness now, she reminded herself bitterly.

The old coaching inn was just as charming as she remembered. Built on four sides of what had once been the coachyard, into which the mail coaches had once driven, the yard had been turned into a delightful enclosed patio, overlooked by the ancient timbered walls of the inn itself.

A smiling receptionist greeted them, and under her professional greeting. Genista saw the flicker of interest in her blue eyes as they lingered on Luke's tautly male features.

'Mr Ferguson. Of course, you booked the suite, didn't you? I'll have someone take up your cases. There's still time for dinner in the main restaurant if you wish, or if you prefer it we could arrange for you to dine in your suite?'

'In our suite, I think,' Luke said decisively. 'We've had a long drive up from the south, and we both feel like relaxing.'

'I'll show you to your suite and have a menu sent up to you straight away,' she promised, with far more enthusiasm than the small task warranted, or so it seemed to Genista. Had she walked into the hotel alone she was quite positive that she wouldn't have merited the same dewy-eyed service.

Their suite of rooms consisted of a delightful sitting room with a beamed ceiling and windows overlooking the courtyard, furnished with charming reproduction antiques; flowers arranged in the empty hearth, plus a large bedroom, dominated by a massive carved fourposter, with a luxurious bathroom off it.

A porter arrived with their luggage while the receptionist was still showing Luke the bedroom, and Genista hung back on the pretext of examining the furniture. She was interested to discover if it had been made by their client, or so she told herself, trying to find excuses for her reluctance to follow Luke into the bedroom. The sight of the huge old-fashioned bed had sent fresh fear crawling through her stomach. When a waiter arrived with a menu she gestured to him to leave it on the coffee table, convinced that she wouldn't be able to touch a morsel of food.

The receptionist left, closing the door behind her. Luke had ordered a meal for both of them, while Genista stood woodenly by the window, trying to control her rising tide of panic. The moment the door closed, like a cell door on a condemned prisoner, her control snapped. She flew to the door, tearing at it in a frenzy, dry sobs rasping her throat.

'Stop it! I've already told you—no hysterics. You won't get round me that way, Genista. I know all about you, remember? A few crocodile tears aren't going to make me change my mind. I've paid dearly for your favours; the highest price a man can pay— I've bought you with my name, and I don't intend to be cheated.'

'You can't do this!'

Her despairing cry was smothered against his chest as he plucked her from the door, hauling her against him so that her body was forced to endure the knowledge of his unashamed arousal.

'I want you, Genista, and I mean to have you.'

'Then you'll have to take me by force,' she told him fiercely, 'because I don't want you, and I never shall.'

'You think not?'

His knowing smile made her feel faintly sick, her

face paling as she realised that there was no way she was going to be able to persuade him to change his mind. For one mad moment she contemplated throwing herself from the window, but this notion was swiftly dispelled. Even had she wanted to, the windows were far too small. Luke was reaching for the phone.

'What are you doing?'

'Cancelling dinner,' he said smoothly. 'I've suddenly realised I have other appetites that need satisfying first. Come here, Genista,' he commanded softly as she started to back away from him. 'There's no need for any games, we both know what it's all about.'

You might do, she wanted to scream, but I don't, but pride held her silent.

She hadn't realised that he was very skilfully backing her towards the open bedroom door, until she felt behind her for the wall and found instead only space. She turned wildly staring at the huge canopied bed.

'Please don't do this, Luke,' she begged passionately. 'Please let me go.'

'It's too late, Genista.' His eyes and mouth were hard—nearly as hard as the fingers gripping her shoulders. 'It was too late from the moment I walked into Greg Hardiman's flat and saw you. If you've any sense you'll meet me half way, but you haven't, have you, so we'll have to do it the hard way. I want you, and nothing is going to stop me taking you—nothing!'

CHAPTER FIVE

HE meant it, Genista realised moments later, half dazed with fear, as Luke lifted her off her feet and carried her through into the bedroom. Her jacket slid off her shoulder as he deposited her on the bed, revealing the pearly skin beneath. He had discarded his jacket and as he followed her on to the bed, the breadth of his shoulders encased in the thin white silk made her catch her breath. In terrified fascination she watched him loosen his tie, wrenching open the top buttons of his shirt, his expression wry as her eyes flickered nervously from the tanned column of his throat to his face.

'You should be doing this,' he told her grimly. 'There's something very erotic about being undressed by one's lover.'

'And you've had lots of practice.' Genista had intended the words to sound disdainful, but instead they were merely breathlessly hesitant. Her stomach was knotted with tension. She wanted to jump off the bed and run to the door—anywhere to get away from the man lounging beside her, his head propped up on one hand as he surveyed the rise and fall of her breasts as her breathing became increasingly agitated—but she could not bear the humiliation of being carried to the bed a second time. Trying to convince herself that the ordeal ahead was just like a particularly nasty dose of medicine, she reasoned that it would be less unpleasant to get it over with as soon as possible

rather than to delay. She had come a long way
from the girl who had thought that she would find
some way of persuading Luke to wait, she acknowledged wryly, glancing up at the man lying
beside her. He ran his hand along her arm, his
fingers spreading possessively over her midriff,
causing her heart to thump erratically with panic.
She could feel the heat of his flesh against her own
even though the flimsy silk separated them. Her
heart seemed to be lodged somewhere in her throat
and she was beginning to feel dizzy with the effort
of appearing calm and uncaring.

'You're an excellent actress,' Luke drawled
smoothly, lifting his hand to push the silky curtain
of her hair behind her ears. 'Looking at you, I
could almost believe this is your first time with a
man, but we both know that isn't true, don't we,
Genista?'

She was beyond words; beyond anything but the
suffocating fear that gripped her as he lowered his
head slowly, his eyes fastening on the soft trembling of her mouth.

His lips felt cool, the pressure of his hands on
her shoulders forcing her backwards against the
pillows. She could feel him sliding the thin straps
of the camisole top over her skin and tensed immediately. His mouth left hers, his eyes searching
her face as he lifted his head.

'Stop it!' he warned her. 'It isn't necessary, and
if you insist on playing silly games you'll force me
to hurt you. You know what I want, Genista,' he
muttered thickly, desire burning hotly in his eyes.
'And I'll make you want it too.'

His hand was on her breast, stroking the flesh
gently over the thin silk. Genista was trembling
from head to foot. Her mouth had gone dry. The

drugging kisses Luke was pressing against her throat and shoulders were triggering off emotions that made her feel a stranger to herself. When his fingers completely released the camisole too, laying bare the pale flesh beneath, she shuddered deeply, trying to pull away, but he flung a leg across her thighs, pinning her to the bed with his superior weight.

'Kiss me, Genista,' he muttered hoarsely against her throat. 'Touch me!' The command was a muttered groan. His forehead was beaded with sweat, his eyes almost black behind their thick fringe of lashes. Genista felt fear pound through her mingled with the first stirrings of an emotion that turned her bones to water. 'Stop tormenting me. You know what I want!'

Her hands were drawn against her will to the hard wall of his chest. Beneath the silk shirt she could feel the crispness of the thick dark hair. Luke moaned and jerked heatedly against her, moving her fingers against the constraining buttons, until the shirt was completely unfastened. Genista trembled violently as he shrugged the shirt off. His skin was faintly flushed, beaded with sweat, and his skin felt hot beneath her fingers. His body clenched as she touched him, and her eyes flew in startled dismay to his face. Dusk was shadowing the room, and in the soft half light she could see quite clearly the structure of the bones lying beneath his skin. She was too bemused by the discovery that the flesh of his shoulders felt like raw silk beneath her fingers to be aware of the fact that he had unzipped her skirt and removed it, until it was too late to stop him.

Embarrassment flooded over her on a hot wave as he held her away from him studying her body, now clad only in her almost transparent briefs.

'You're even more beautiful than I imagined,' he said slowly, and then almost reverendly lowered his head, touching his lips first to one tender rose-tipped breast and then the other. A sensation not unlike a sudden shaft of pain spread hotly through her, followed by a tumultuous clamor of excitement, so strong that it swept away her self-consciousness. Sensations she had never dreamed existed carried her along in their fast-flowing flood. She gasped as she felt Luke's mouth against her breast a second time, shuddering mindlessly as her nipple hardened betrayingly beneath the expert stimulus of his tongue. Pleasure mingled with pain in a feeling so intense that it blotted out everything but the need to place her arms round Luke's neck and hold his head captive against her body.

When he eventually lifted his head they were both breathing hard. His fingers cupped her breasts and fierce longing stirred deep inside her. So this was desire, she thought hazily, scarcely believing the sensations he was awakening within her body. Her mind seemed unable to control her wanton flesh. It clung and pleaded, mutely enticing Luke's touch, until she was sighing softly with the pleasure he could evoke. Only when he started to remove his trousers did reality reassert itself. Shocked by the abandon with which she had responded to him, Genista took advantage of his momentary withdrawal to stumble off the bed.

'Genista?'

'I wanted to take a shower.' It was the first excuse that came into her head. Anything to get away from him and have a few minutes to herself in which to come to terms with this sensual side of her nature she had never dreamed she possessed. It was as though Luke's touch had unlocked all the doors behind which she had hidden away all her natural urges. In his arms she became primitive woman, and the knowledge shocked her profoundly.

Luke's fingers curled round her wrist. He was watching her with a hungry intensity that brought fresh colour to her skin. The expression in his eyes was so explicit that it set off a traitorous response deep within her own nerve centres. Her stomach went weak with longing.

'Later,' he said softly. 'We'll take one together, but right now, I've got other things on my mind.' His tug on her wrist caught her off guard and she half fell on top of him, her small protest lost beneath the fierce pressure of his mouth as it closed over hers, banishing for ever any doubts she might have had about the intensity of his desire for her.

'Touch me, Genista,' he said thickly. 'Make love to me the way you made love to Bob.'

Her hands were placed against the hard wall of his chest, the dark hair which arrowed down towards his navel, slightly rough against her palms. She could feel the fierce pulsating tide of his desire, his thigh muscles bunched with tension as he forced her back against the bed. His thumb stroking roughly over her throbbing nipples, increasing her overwhelming need for complete fulfilment. She had never known that sexual desire could be like this; rising on a spiralling tide of excitement strong enough to sweep aside everything that stood in its path until there was nothing but sensation, her body so perfectly attuned to Luke's that she responded to him without conscious volition.

It was like riding an Atlantic roller, headily exciting and frighteningly dangerous, but Genista

didn't heed the fear; her fingers, seemingly of
their own free will, were making urgent forays
against the male flesh beneath them, Luke's harshly
indrawn breath inciting her to stroke shy fingers
over the flat plane of his stomach; and have her
mouth possessed until she could no longer breathe,
as a punishment for her temerity. All conscious
thought was suspended; there was only the urgent
clamourings of her own body; the desire to know
Luke's complete possession driving her to the point
where her thighs parted willingly beneath him, her
breath sobbing in her throat as she felt the first
powerful thrust of his body against her. His mouth
closed over hers, teasing her lips apart and sliding
moistly against the soft inner flesh abandoned to
him.

Small, animal cries died unuttered under the
pressure of his kiss, her arms winding tightly round
his neck as she arched instinctively beneath him.
Almost unable to bear the fiercely rising crescendo
of longing he was arousing, she dug her nails
mindlessly into the smooth muscles of his back,
and then just when she thought she must surely die
from the sheer agony of wanting him, pain tore
through her, obliterating the mists of desire which
had clouded her mind, and forcing her to accept
that not only had she responded, but that she had
actually incited Luke to possess her.

The frantic cry of pain she was unable to suppress stilled him instantly. Through the darkness
she could feel him watching her. Every muscle of
the body which only seconds before had melted
against him in mute invitation was now tensed
against his intrusion. The arms she had wrapped
around him, holding him to her, lay stiffly at her
side, her face turned away so that he would not see

the betraying sparkle of her tears. The only sound to break the silence was their own breathing, tortured and laborious, and she was filled with a searing sense of shame. How could she have responded so freely; so—so wantonly? She shuddered deeply and heard Luke swear, his hand sliding along her throat to cup her face and turn it towards him.

He seemed about to say something, and Genista stared helplessly back at him. Her heart was thudding so loudly she felt sure he must hear it. Her mouth had gone dry, and she felt sick with the knowledge of how she had betrayed her ideals.

'Oh God!' She caught the smothered words as Luke's arms tightened round her, her protests lost beneath his mouth as the last barriers of innocence were torn away, and pain gave way to a renewal of her earlier urgency. Above her she could hear Luke breathing harshly, his muttered, 'Relax ... God knows I don't want to hurt you,' impinging somewhere on her outer consciousness before the same mindless pleasure she had known before engulfed her, and she was responding to Luke's possession with fevered moans.

'Love me, Luke ... please love me ...' She heard the words with shocking clarity, but they hardly seemed to matter any longer. Luke was teaching her the true meaning of the word pleasure, and her whole body was coming truly alive for the first time. The world spun dizzily round her, filled with exploding stars and vivid waves of pleasure so intense that they blotted out everything else completely.

It was only later, when pleasure had given way to exhaustion, that those moaned words returned to torment her. Luke was lying on his side next to her, one arm curved possessively round her waist, his breathing faintly ragged. She turned away, bewildered and shocked by the way he had aroused her, tremblingly aware that while her mind detested him her body had welcomed him as though he were the lover it had always dreamed of.

'Why in God's name didn't you tell me the truth?'

She tried to turn away, but he wouldn't let her. He raised himself on one a elbow, winding his fingers into her hair so that she was forced to look at him.

'I don't know what you mean.'

It was a stupid thing to say, and she regretted it instantly. His eyes flared bitterly. She had seen him angry before, but never as angry as this.

'Liar! You know damned well what I mean. Why did you let me think you were Bob's mistress, when all the time . . .' He broke off, and Genista was appalled to see how white he was, the bones of his face standing out beneath the tanned skin.

'Why didn't you tell me you were a virgin; that you'd never known a man? Surely to God you must have known . . .'

'Known what?' Genista asked tonelessly. 'All I knew was that you were threatening me.'

'And so you abandoned yourself to me? Why? Were you hoping to punish me? To make me feel guilt?'

'I wanted to protect Bob,' Genista said in the same low voice. 'You were threatening to tell Elaine that we were having an affair, and I couldn't let you do that.'

'But you weren't, were you?' His fingers suddenly tightened hurtingly in her hair, his expression unreadable as he forced her to look up at him.

'Were you thinking of *him* when I made love to you? Wishing I were him?'

'Does it matter?' Her voice sounded oddly thick with the tears she was trying to suppress. 'Does anything matter any longer?'

'You cared that much about him?'

'He's my friend,' Genista said simply, no longer caring whether he believed her or not.

She didn't have the right to tell him about Elaine's operation, and besides, all she really wanted to do was simply to fall asleep and perhaps for a few hours find escape from the tormenting memory of how her body had betrayed her. It was useless trying to persuade herself that she had not experienced pleasure, that Luke had not taken her to the highest peaks of human experience, and she writhed mentally to think about it. She tried to pull away from him and winced slightly, shrinking as she felt the anger burn up inside him. It was all wrong; she was the one who ought to be experiencing resentment; she was the one who had been wronged.

'You're angry with me?'

His mouth tightened ominously. 'Angry?' He stared incredulously at her. 'Of course I'm damned well angry! You were a virgin. You don't know the first thing about making love, and yet you let me . . . Sheer frustration brought me the closest I've ever come to rape. I thought you were playing with me. But that doesn't make me feel any better.'

'We could have the marriage annulled.'

'No!' The denial was decisive. 'You've already made a laughing stock of me once; I'm not giving you a second chance. And besides, as you said yourself, Bob loves his wife. No, Genista. We're

married and that's the way we're going to stay,
although God knows not many marriages can have
a worse start.' He was staring into her face as
though he was searching for something.

'Lord knows how I missed it. You're as innocent
as a child, and it's written all over you. So why the
big act at the party?'

'I didn't like the way you looked at me.'

'And how did I look at you?'

'As though . . . as though . . .'

'As though I were imagining what it would be
like to go to bed with you? And for that you put
us both through all this?'

There was more to it than that, but Genista was
feeling too confused and sleepy to argue. It had
been his air of calm arrogance, his confident assurance that she was his for the taking, which had
infuriated her.

'I didn't want to marry you,' she said.

'But you did—for the sake of a man who wasn't
even your lover, but I warn you, Genista, I won't
have any ghost making up an unseen third in my
bed. We're married.'

'You hurt me!'

The childish cry was born of a desire to punish
him for teaching her body to defy her, but she
hadn't been prepared for the way his eyes
darkened, his mouth compressing as he released
her.

'It was inevitable,' he said curtly, 'and the price
you paid for your own stupidity. If you'd told me
that you'd never been with a man before . . .'

'You would have what?'

'There are ways and ways, Genista. I thought
your experience matched my own, and I wanted
you so badly that I wasn't in the mood for the

kind of loveplay that would have made things easier for you.'

Her cheeks burned at his frankness and she was glad of the darkness to hide her blushes.

'Go to sleep,' Luke told her brusquely. 'We'll talk in the morning.'

To her amazement she slept quite well, although it was still early when she awoke. The unfamiliar weight of Luke's arm across her body puzzled her at first, until the events of the previous evening came rushing back with shattering clarity. Her body felt strange, lethargic and oddly boneless, almost as though it no longer belonged exclusively to her.

Luke was lying next to her, the dark beginnings of a beard shadowing his jaw. In sleep he looked younger, a faint flush lying along his cheekbones, thick, dark lashes fanning the delicate skin beneath his eyes. Genista suppressed an alien urge to lean across and touch him, subduing the need to know more about this man with whom she had experienced nature's most intimate bond. He stirred in his sleep and she froze in horror as the sheet slipped from his shoulders revealing the scratches along his back. Vividly she remembered digging her nails into his firm flesh as waves of ecstasy swept her, and she dragged her eyes away from the sight of his torn skin, shuddering with revulsion to think that she had acted so primitively.

His arm lay just below her breasts, reminding her of the intimacy with which he had touched her—and how much she had wanted him to touch her, his hands and lips exploring every inch of her satin flesh.

Unable to bear her thoughts any longer, she pushed aside the bedclothes and slithered away

from his constraining arm. Gathering up clean
underclothes, she headed for the bathroom, ignoring the bath in favour of the benefits of a brisk
shower. Her shower gel was in her case, and she
tiptoed stealthily back into the bedroom, not
wanting to wake Luke. Vague thoughts of leaving
the hotel before he awoke crossed her mind. She
had no fears now that he would say anything to
Elaine—how could he? He knew quite well that
she and Bob had never been intimate, but she could
not make a move until she had cleansed her body
from the memories of last night.

Turning the spray on fully, she was too busily
engrossed in lathering herself to hear the soft foot-
fall on the tile floor, and it was only the closing of
the bathroom door that alerted her to the fact that
she was no longer alone. She looked up and saw
Luke leaning against the closed door, arms folded
across his bare chest, a brief towelling robe belted
loosely round his waist.

'Trying to wash away the taint of my touch?' he
jeered unpleasantly. 'It won't work. They say that
the memory of her first lover is something a woman
carries with her all her life.'

'I just wanted a shower.' Her towel was lying on
the floor out of reach, and she wished desperately
that she had the courage to reach for the shower
curtain and pull it between them. Luke was studying her body with something closely akin to clinical
detachment, and it didn't help remembering how
he had touched it the previous night. To her shame
and horror Genista felt her breasts swell slightly as
though aroused by his glance.

'So that you could feel "clean" again before you
left me? That's what you were planning, wasn't it?
We're staying together, Genista. I've already told

you, no one makes a fool of me twice. I won't have people saying that my wife walked out on me after one night of wedded bliss. If you leave me, I'll tell Elaine you and Bob were having an affair. Oh, I know it's not true, but she obviously doesn't, otherwise you would never have agreed to marry me in the first place. I don't know why you're so anxious to protect his marriage, but if the fear of destroying it is what it takes to keep you at my side, then destroy it I will, if you ever try to leave.'

'But we can't live together!' Genista was aghast. He might as well condemn them both to a life senteance in prison.

'Why not? Because I took your virginity? Because I "hurt" you? If that's what's bothering you—and I suspect it is, perhaps now's a good time to show you that there doesn't have to be pain.'

He had removed his robe before Genista could gather her scattered wits. The foaming gel she had been lathering into her skin adhered to him as he reached for her, but instead of lifting her out of the shower, he began a slow caressing movement over her back, stroking the tense muscles, until they began to relax against her will. His fingers rested lightly against her waist for a moment, before descending further to explore the narrow curves of her hips. The nerves in her stomach quivered protestingly, wanting to deny the power of those arousing hands, but already the weak, melting sensation she remembered from last night was spreading upwards from her thighs. Luke's fingers against the sensitive chord of her spine making her shiver with mingled pleasure and fear.

'I see you're one of those old-fashioned girls who doesn't believe in sunbathing in the nude? Last night I thought it was merely another carefully designed ploy to arouse and tease—all men enjoy the thrill of thinking they're the first, whether it's seeing or touching—and I got both, didn't I?'

She wanted to deny it, but his lips were tracing butterfly-light kisses along her throat, his thumb stroking the acutely sensitive skin behind her small ear. She was trembling as though gripped by some tropical fever, her eyes drawn irresistibly to the tanned flesh of Luke's body, which proclaimed all too obviously that he did not believe in undue modesty when it came to a suntan.

'I know you want to touch me.' The calm words panicked her, then Luke's hand cupped her chin. 'It's nothing to be ashamed of. It's only natural to want to give pleasure as well as to receive it. Your skin tastes of peaches.' He bit her flesh delicately, his hands sliding down to her waist to hold her against him. She lifted a hand to push him away, but it was wet and slipperly from the gel and slid impotently over his skin. The impact of his muscled body beneath her palm triggered off the same desire she had experienced earlier that morning to discover more about him.

'Genista?'

She looked upwards. Luke's fingers tangled in her hair, holding the base of her skull so that his lips were given licence to plunder the vulnerable line of hers. Only this time there was no force in the kisses, only a tormentingly teasing provocation that promised and withheld, until she had forgotton that this was a man whom she professed to hate and wanted only to prolong the briefly tantalising pressure of his kiss until it hardened and demanded the way it had done last night. Her small moan of frustration as once again his lips were withdrawn after the briefest of caresses impelled her to reach upwards, clasping her fingers behind Luke's neck, her body pressed against him so that the next time his mouth touched hers she could prevent him from depriving her of its contact. His shoulders felt sleekly smooth beneath her questing fingers, and when this time his kiss fulfilled its earlier promise, probing and tasting all the inner sweetness of her mouth, her hands moved urgently against his skin, exploring, and learning every tautly male contour, until her roaming fingers were captured and held against his chest, rasped by the thick curling body hair darkening the tanned flesh.

'You're learning, but I came in here to take a shower, not make love.' He reached behind her for the soap and she was filled by the most ridiculous sense of deprivation. What was the matter with her? she chided herself. She ought to be feeling relieved, not ... not ... She struggled for a moment, but then her innate sense of honesty surfaced and she was forced to admit the truth— she was disappointed; bitterly disappointed because Luke did not want to continue making love to her!

She moved away blindly, and heard him laugh softly above her. 'Where do you think you're going? I told you last night we'd take a shower together, and that's exactly what we're going to do.'

'I don't want to.'

'But you're going to anyway.'

He was already soaping himself, and she followed the action mindlessly, her tongue wetting suddenly dry lips as she watched the sleek play of his muscles beneath his skin.

'Now you try.' Her hands were suddenly caught and placed against his body, his eyes mocking her shocked expression as he said softly, 'You were managing okay when I walked in here. If it helps just close your eyes and try to remind yourself I'm still a human being, even if I am a slightly different shape.'

Slightly! Genista told herself that it was fastidious disgust that coiled through her as she massaged soap reluctantly against his skin, but when his own hands brought a shuddering response from her own body as they stroked and caressed with a surety that spoke of long experience she could deny the truth no longer. Each caress was punctuated with a kiss, each kiss gradually deepening in intensity until she herself was pressing feverish kisses against Luke's throat and shoulders. Not even the fine spray of the shower rinsing away the soap broke the spell Luke's touch had aroused. When he carried her to the bed, she felt only an aching need for him to prolong his lovemaking. All her inhibitions seemed to have vanished. She responded feverishly to the touch of his hands and lips, moaning softly as his hands cupped her breasts, swollen with desire. The pain of the previous night was forgotton.

'Say it, Genista,' Luke demanded harshly, when the convulsive arching of her body beneath him betrayed her growing need. 'Tell me you want me.'

'I want you.'

She gasped a little at the fierceness of his kiss and then responded to it, losing herself in the sensations building up inside her in intensity until she was matching him step for step, his possession a welcome relief after the aching emptiness she had been experiencing.

This time there was no pain, only a gradual build-up to pleasure so prolonged that Luke's

name had become a mindless refrain on her tongue
smothered by the hard pressure of his mouth as
they clung together in mutual abandonment.

'Don't ever try to tell me we're not sexually
compatible at least,' Luke said roughly when it was
over. 'You might love Bob, but I'm the one who
can arouse you to the point where nothing matters
other than that I possess you completely.'

It was several seconds before Genista realised
that Luke thought she loved Bob. It was on the tip
of her tongue to correct him when some sixth sense
warned her not to. What she felt for him was only
desire, of course; how could it be anything else,
and yet deep down inside her she knew that she
could never have responded so abandonedly to any
man she did not love. Love? For Luke? But that
was ridiculous. Was it? a small voice questioned.
Wasn't it possible that all her initial aggression and
fear of him had been sparked off by a primitive
need for self-preservation? Hadn't she known instinctively then that in some way he threatened her
peace of mind; represented the sort of danger she
had promised herself she had left behind with
Richard?

But she couldn't love Luke. Why not? that same
small voice asked calmly.

It couldn't possibly be true. She refused to believe it. It was sexual desire, that was all. She closed
her eyes, letting sleep wash over her. She dreamed
of Luke and awoke with damp eyes to find him
sitting in a chair by the window reading a paper.

'Do you often cry in your sleep?'

'I don't know.' He looked so savagely angry that
she felt frightened. The fact that he was dressed
while she lay naked beneath the protective sheets
made her feel at a disadvantage.

'Oh, for God's sake don't look at me like that! Dream of Bob if you must, but I warn you, Genista, if I ever think you're dreaming of him when you're in my arms, I'll take my pleasure from you as a man does with a woman he's bought for the night!'

She flinched as he flung the paper down and walked towards the door. 'I'm going out for a walk. I'll be back for lunch. And remember, this marriage stands for just as long as I want it to.'

When he had gone Genista cried as she had not done even when they brought the news of her parents' death. Not for Bob, but for herself, because when she dreamed of Luke she had dreamed that she had been begging him to make love to her, and he had turned his back on her, jeering that love was the last emotion he would feel for her. Alone she faced the truth. She loved him and must have done so, unknowingly right from the start. A deep shudder went right through her. She could only pray that he tired of her quickly, before she betrayed her feelings to him. His mockery of her love was something she could not endure. Sexually compatible, he had called them, but she knew that her body's response was that of a woman deeply in love with the man who possesses her. She loved him! If only she had discovered this before they had married. Wild horses would not have dragged her to the altar had she done so, but it was too late now. They were married. She was Luke's wife. The woman he had married purely because he wanted to possess her; the woman he had thought the property of another man. For the first time she bitterly regretted her lack of experience. With it she might have known how best to hold his interest, perhaps even fan it so that he never grew bored with her. She was being ridiculous, she told herself. Desire was no sound basis for marriage. It would wane eventually, it was bound to do so. And she would be left with nothing. No, not nothing—she would have a broken heart.

CHAPTER SIX

THE morning dragged by. Had she been on her own Genista might have entertained herself by taking a walk through the glorious Lakeland countryside, but she was not alone. Her eyes kept straying to the window which overlooked the wooded hillside, but there was no sign of Luke.

Where had he gone when he left their room? The thought of her response to his lovemaking brought a fresh stab of pain. How could she have been so blind to her own danger? How could she not have realised what was happening to her? In a less worldly age she might have described her feelings for him as 'love at first sight', but because such naïveté was the object of mockery amongst her contemporaries, she had wilfully deceived herself that the immediate awareness she had felt had been strong dislike. How could any woman who professed to dislike a man respond to his lovemaking the way she had responded to Luke?

He returned shortly before lunch; a meal which was eaten almost completely in silence.

'I've decided that we might as well return to London,' he announced abruptly when they had been served with their coffee. Something had happened during his walk to change him. The eyes which rested on her averted profile were completely impersonal, his attitude towards her that of a coolly polite stranger. No longer did the burning intensity of his gaze trigger off shivers of awareness, scorching her flesh where it alighted upon it. He smiled mirthlessly, lifting his cup to his mouth. 'It wasn't my original intention, but in the circumstances it seems the best course of action—for both of us.'

Genista went upstairs to pack, leaving Luke to settle their bill. She had closed her own case and was staring at his, wondering whether her newly married status meant that he would expect her to adopt the duties of a normal wife, when he walked in, calmly settling the matter for her by opening the wardrobe and withdrawing the clothes he had hung there. He packed methodically, with a precision that spoke of long practice. No doubt in the early days of building up his business he must have travelled widely, and probably not always alone.

Jealousy knifed agonisingly through her. How many other women had known the pleasure she had found in his arms? It was something she would be wiser not to think about, but it was impossible not to. How many of them had he loved? Or had there only been one—Verity? Verity who had gone off with his brother-in-law because she preferred being a rich man's mistress to a poor man's wife.

'Ready?'

She nodded numbly, following him out of the room. On the threshold she was unable to resist one backward glance. In these impersonal surroundings she had come to full womanhood; had experienced ecstasy and pain; had learned the difference between mere infatuation—which was what she had felt for Richard—and love.

It was late afternoon when they reached the out-skirts of London. Luke had said not one word about their future together, and Genista felt as though her forehead was in the grip of an iron band, which tightened increasingly painfully as the silence between them stretched into a tension that plucked at her overwrought nerve ends.

'I want to call at the office,' Luke told her as he turned off the motorway. 'There are some papers I want to pick up.'

Everything was the same—but different. It was hard to believe that the last time she had entered these offices she had entered them as a single woman, unaware of what lay ahead of her.

Bob looked up from his desk as they walked in. Most of the staff had already left, and he did a double-take as he saw them.

'We weren't expecting you back. How did it go?'

Jilly walked out of her office, and grinned at them. Luke asked her if she could get him a file, and while they talked, Genista managed to ask Bob about Elaine. His face was grave.

'She has to have major surgery. The surgeon wants to be sure that they remove the growth com-pletely.' He looked close to tears, and Genista laid a sympathetic hand on his arm, feeling almost maternal.

'They can do wonderful things these days,' she comforted him.

He smiled bleakly. 'I know. It isn't the operation I'm worried about—it's afterwards—when Elaine realises what it means. I had to give consent for the operation. Before she went in she begged me not to let them remove her . . . anything, but the surgeon told me that if they didn't she could die.

Oh God, Genista!' He covered his face with his hands, his shoulders bowed and shaking, and Genista placed her arms round him instinctively, putting her cheek comfortingly against his hair.

'You've done the right thing, I'm sure of it. The operation will be a shock to her, but once she realises that you still love her, that you still feel the same . . .'

'Of course I do.' Bob's voice was rough. 'Love isn't something you turn on and off like a tap.'

'Have you told Bob our good news?'

Neither of them had heard Luke approach the desk. Genista looked up, frightened by the black fury in his eyes. How he must hate her, now that he had discovered the truth. He had thought her a sophisticated woman of the world, well schooled in everything it took to please a man, instead of which he had discovered that she was an inexperienced virgin. No wonder he was looking at her as though he wanted to murder her!

'What news?' Jilly asked gaily, coming to join them. 'Don't tell me you've finally got Genista to declare a truce in this war she's declared against the male sex.'

'I hope so,' Luke replied dryly, 'otherwise it doesn't say much for the success of our marriage.'

'Marriage!' Bob and Jilly uttered the word in disbelieving unison. 'You're married? Oh, Genista, how could you without telling me?' Jilly wailed. 'I want to know all about it. What did you wear? When was it all decided? You dark horse, you, spinning me that line about disliking Luke, and all the time . . . Do you know, she even had me convinced that she didn't know how you felt about her,' she complained to Luke. 'But I could see that you'd fallen for her like a ton of bricks the moment you set eyes on her.'

'Perceptive of you.'

Was she the only one who was aware of the sarcastic inflection behind the words? Genista wondered miserably. Jilly's ecstatic chatter filled the awkward silence Luke's announcement had provoked. Bob congratulated them stiltedly, and Genista knew that his thoughts were on Elaine. Poor Bob! She wished there was some way she could help him.

'You'll be giving up your job, of course?' Jilly mused. 'Does Luke have a flat in London? Nice, but hardly suitable for children,' she added, betraying quite plainly the direction her thoughts were taking.

'You're ahead of us there,' Luke responded lightly. 'But as it happens I don't live in London. I have a house about fifty miles away. It's in the country, and the pleasure of returning to it after a day cooped up in an office more than makes up for the travelling involved.'

'And now it will be even more pleasurable because you'll have Genista to go home to,' Jilly murmured. 'You've always loved the country, haven't you, Gen? She's a small town girl at heart—but then I expect you already know that?'

'We haven't had a lot of time to catch up on each other's backgrounds,' Luke replied succinctly. 'We've been too involved with more immediate concerns.'

Jilly laughed delightedly when Genista coloured.

'Well, I think it's wonderful. My only complaint is that I didn't get an invitation to the wedding.'

'It was a very quiet ceremony,' Genista told her

quietly. 'We were married by Luke's godfather, in the Lake District.'

'What did you wear?' Jilly demanded. 'I want to know all the details.'

'A pale green silk suit,' Luke said promptly before Genista could answer. His arm circled her waist, holding her against him, the look in his eyes full of tenderness as he added softly, 'And very beautiful she looked in it too.'

It was only to keep up appearances, of course, but even so, her heart pounded with dizzy pleasure for a briefly betraying moment before she reminded herself sternly that it meant nothing.

'Green silk? Oh, not that gorgeous outfit you bought the other week, Gen?' Jilly exclaimed. 'The one you were going to wear for the christening?'

Genista could feel Luke watching her, and the tiny scraps of paper which had once been his cheque seemed to burn a hole in her handbag.

'Thrifty as well as beautiful!'

The light words held an undercurrent of steel that made Genista dread the time when they were alone. Luke had specified that she was not to wear clothes paid for by anyone else, and neither had she done, so why should he be annoyed because she had not used his cheque?

'You're very quiet, Bob?'

Genista frowned a little at the challenge in the quietly spoken words. Was Luke trying subtly to remind her of the weapon he still held? He need not have done.

'Old age creeping up on me, I suppose,' Bob replied lightly. 'Genista knows I wish her all the happiness in the world. She deserves it, and I suspect it's very selfish of me to worry about how I'm going to replace her.'

'Very,' Luke agreed coolly. 'But I'm afraid you'll have to. Genista will have more than enough to do running our home, and no newly married man wants to find his wife dropping with exhaustion every evening.'

The pointed comment made Genista's cheeks burn. Jilly winked at her and hissed conspiratorially, 'Lucky thing! What I wouldn't give to be waiting for Luke to come home to me every night!'

They left shortly afterwards. Luke tossed the files he had collected on to the back seat of the Maserati as he opened the passenger door.

This time the silence between them seemed to have an added ingredient of hostility, and Genista's head began to throb painfully with the tension gripping her body.

They drove east, along the M4 in the direction of Bath, the countryside rolling and unfamiliar. Some forty miles outside London Luke took a slip road off the motorway and in the gathering dusk Genista gained only a vague impression of high hedges and narrow winding roads.

Luke switched on the cassette player and the strains of Debussy filled the car. Genista tried to relax her tense muscles, but it was impossible. The intimacy of the car seemed to close over her, like a thick, muffling blanket. Luke, on the other hand, appeared completely relaxed. She stole a look at his remote profile. He was concentrating on the road ahead, but the anger which had seemed to grip him as they left the office had gone. His shirt was open at the throat and memories of how his body had felt beneath her urgent fingers poured over her.

'What's wrong? Have I suddenly grown another head?'

She looked away quickly, hating herself for being

caught out staring at him. She was like a miser, greedily studying his gold, storing up memories for the time when he might no longer be able to look upon the real article.

They were deep in the country. In front of them a Tudor farmhouse materialised out of the dusk, the black and white façade of the upper storeys picked out by the new moon.

The house had an air of serenity that soothed Genista's bruised heart. It seemed to reach out and embrace her, and she wondered idly to whom it belonged. Some rich landowner, no doubt. From the front it resembled an 'E' without the middle, the two outer wings like arms protecting the main body of the building.

As Maserati purred throatily towards the locked gates she started in surprise. Luke flicked a switch inside the car and they opened automatically. This time Genista did not look away when he returned her stare.

'*This* is your home?'

'Well, I'm certainly not taking you to someone else's.'

'But . . . but it's beautiful,' she said weakly.

His smile mocked her confusion. 'What did you expect? Some Victorian monstrosity tarted up by a fashionable interior designer? I saw this house for the first time twenty years ago when I was still at school, and I vowed then that one day it would be mine. You could call it a case of love at first sight.'

'I'm surprised you believe in such things.'

The words slipped out, tinged with pain. Such a short time ago she wouldn't have believed in it herself, but now she knew better.

'But then you don't really know me, do you?' Luke said coolly. 'Love isn't something that happens according to plan. It obeys no laws but its own. Surely you must have noticed how incongruously it strikes? How ... cruelly? After all, that's something you've had first-hand experience of yourself, isn't it?'

For a moment Genista thought he had guessed how she felt about him. Her face went paper-white, her lips parting tremulously in quick denial, and then she realised that he was probably referring to her parents. He couldn't know how she felt; she had been at such pains to hide it from him.

He stopped the car in front of the house, gravel crunching underfoot as he walked round to her door and opened it for her.

The house was all in darkness. '

'Someone comes in to clean for me every morning, and leave a meal prepared if I'm dining at home, but I prefer not to have live-in help. I enjoy my privacy.'

He touched a light switch and the square hall was immediately illuminated with light. Genista stared around, her eyes widening with pleasure. The hall was panelled, the wood glowing mellowly with the patina of the years. Underfoot on the parquet floor lay silky Persian rugs, glowing richly. On a table beneath a portrait stood a huge brass bowl full of crimson roses.

'The sitting room is through there,' Luke murmured, touching her arm. 'It's the library really, but I prefer it to the drawing room, which I find too large when I'm on my own. I left instructions for a buffet meal to be left for us. I'll just go and bring in the cases.'

Genista was in the library, examining some of the books on the shelves when he returned. The room was furnished comfortably rather than luxuriously, and she had an immediate sense of being at home.

'I expect you do a good deal of business entertaining here,' she commented when Luke walked in.

He shrugged off his jacket and walked over to a glass-fronted cabinet removing a bottle and two glasses.

'This is my home, not a conference centre,' he told her harshly as he poured the golden amber liquid into the crystal. 'I didn't buy the house as a tax deductible investment, if that's what you mean. When I want to do business I use my office—that's what it's for. When I want to relax I come home. It may be that I have to call upon you occassionally to entertain for me, but it will be occasionally— you won't have to work for your keep if that's what's worrying you. And talking about "keep".' He picked up one of the glasses and brought it across to her. 'Malt whisky—drink it, you look pale, it will do you good ... For the duration of our marriage I'll make you an allowance. Although I don't expect you to act as my social secretary, you will have certain ... responsibilities. You'll need clothes ...'

'I don't want your money!' Genista put down her glass, its contents untouched, her voice tight with anger. 'I have plenty of money for my wants. I don't want yours, Luke.'

'But nevertheless you will take it.' A muscle twitched in his jaw, and his fingers were clenched round the precious crystal. 'You destroyed the cheque I gave you to buy a wedding outfit—your pride refused to allow you to wear something I had paid for. Well, I have my pride too, Genista, and just as long as you're my wife, *I* will keep you. Is that understood?'

For a moment she contemplated defying him, but the look in his eyes warned her that it would be wiser not to.

'I suppose I'll be allowed to keep my car,' she responded sarcastically at length.

'What would you do if I said "no?" Keep within the bounds of this house like a prisoner rather than touch anything I might have given you? I don't carry the plague, you know, Genista. I won't contaminate you.'

'You already have.'

She said it so quietly that she thought he hadn't heard her, until the brittle sound of glass breaking brought her head up in shocked protest. His glass lay shattered in the hearth in a dozen pieces, his face white with fury.

'Damn you, you won't let me forget, will you?' he swore. 'What am I supposed to do? Pay a penance for the rest of my life because I took your virginity? What is it you hate the most, Genista? The fact that I wasn't Bob, or the fact that you enjoyed it, despite that?'

'You're dispicable!'

'Despicable or not, I'm still your husband. Remember that, won't you?'

When the door slammed behind him Genista sank into the nearest chair. She heard the throaty roar of the Maserati as it roared away, although it was several seconds before she realised that Luke had left her completely alone in her new home. She waited half an hour and when he did not return she rose on shaky legs and started to explore her new surroundings.

Across the hall from the library was the drawing room, a beautifully proportioned room, which had obviously been remodelled during the Georgian era. The high, moulded ceiling and graceful marble fireplace drew a faint sigh of appreciation from her. The room was decorated in shades of palest green, and beautiful though it was she could quite see why Luke might prefer the library for relaxing in. It was much more a family room. A family! She stopped like someone transfixed. Where on earth were her errant thoughts leading? Any family that filled this beautiful house would not be hers and Luke's, but the thought of the children he might father on another woman left her raw with a pain that lacerated her already tender heart.

Behind the library was a formal dining room, elegant antique furniture gleaming under the lights of the chandelier. Genista closed the double doors quietly, trying not to imagine that huge mahogany table filled with a large family.

The kitchen had been completely modernised, but in a way that completely kept its traditional appeal. There was a note on the table saying that a salad and a cooked chicken had been left in the fridge.

Genista did not feel hungry. Her ears were alert for the first sound of the returning Maserati. When it did not come she went back to the library, reluctant to explore upstairs, as though she were a visitor who must await the invitation of the owner.

She was curled up asleep in a chair in the library, when something wakened her. She stiffened, tensing as she heard the front door open, and slow footsteps crossing the hall. The door handle turned, and she held her breath. It was gone two o'clock in the morning. Where had Luke been?

He opened the door and stood by it, swaying slightly, his eyes glittering dangerously over her sleepy features.

'Waiting for me like a dutiful wife?' His voice was faintly slurred, and alarm clawed at Genista as she realised that he had been drinking.

'Why, I wonder? Not because you were lonely in bed without me? Or was it? You wanted me this morning, Genista, no matter how much those flashing eyes of yours want to deny it. Oh, you're safe enough now,' he muttered. 'There's a certain something to be said for alcohol—it blunts one's desire. Shocked?' His raw mockery caught at her nerves. 'You ought to be grateful that you're being spared my unwanted advances; that I'm not defiling you by further exhibitions of my lust. You hate me, don't you? Don't you?' he demanded ferociously. 'I took your virginity, and you haven't got the guts to admit that you enjoyed the experience, so instead you blame me—hating me.'

'If you'll just tell me which is my room.' She daren't provoke him any further by retaliating. He was in a dangerously volatile mood, and even in the knowledge of her love, she shuddered at the thought of how he might use her in his present savage mood.

'Take your pick. You can even share mine, but you won't want to do that, will you, Genista? Who knows, you might actually turn to me one fine night and behave like a woman, and that would never do, would it? No one must be allowed to touch what's being sacrificed on the altar to your love for Bob. You stupid little fool!' His voice roughened suddenly, his hands grasping her shoulders and wrenching her out of the chair. 'Are you going to spend the whole of your life in love with a man who doesn't want you?'

Genista looked him straight in the eyes.

'Yes.'

After all, it was the truth, but the man she loved wasn't Bob. It was Luke. He let her go without a word. Her case was too heavy to carry upstairs, so she unzipped it and removed the silk cheongsam; too exhausted to search through it for anything else. The dress would do as a robe. All she wanted to do was to sleep—and to forget.

The first door she opened revealed a bedroom decorated in strongly male colours, and even without the silk dressing gown on the bed she would have guessed it was Luke's. She closed the door, her heart hammering with pain and went to the room farthest away from his and switched on the light.

It was obviously a guestroom, decorated prettily in soft pinks, with its own private bathroom. Genista undressed quickly, showering briefly before sliding beneath the cool cotton sheets.

A telephone ringing somewhere woke her. Someone must have answered it, because the shrill sound was cut off in mid-peal. She opened her eyes and looked round. The sun was streaming in through her window. She climbed out of bed and crossed over to it, pulling aside the curtains to stare out at the lovingly restored Elizabethan gardens below.

'Genista!' There was a brief tap on the door and she barely had time to pull on her silk robe before Luke walked in.

He was already dressed in jeans and a thin cotton shirt, all signs of the previous evening's drinking gone.

'That was my sister on the phone,' he announced without preamble. 'She's heard about our wedding from Amy, and she's on her way over to see us.

She should be here later this afternoon. Apparently a crisis has blown up.'

His eyes were on the silk robe, and Genista had the feeling that for a moment something had made him forget completely what he had been about to say. Seconds later she knew the reason why.

'It's Lucy's half term, and Marina wants us to look after her. When you get to know my sister better you'll come to realise that she has a blithe disregard of other people's plans, but when it comes to roping them into hers ... but on this occasion I feel I owe it to her to help. Philip's been in touch with her. He wants her back.' He turned away abruptly, and Genista had no difficulty in guessing where his thoughts lay. Barely forty-eight hours after he had tied himself to her he had learned that the woman he really loved was free. Perhaps she had found after all that mere wealth did not make up for love; or perhaps Verity had come to realise that with Luke she could have both! The bitchiness of the thought dismayed her.

'Marina isn't sure how Lucy will take it. It's her own damned silly fault, I warned her about not pumping Lucy's head full of silly tales about her father, but Marina wouldn't listen. Now she's afraid Lucy will reject Philip. The situation between them is still at a very difficult stage, and she feels that she and Philip need time alone together.'

'I expect she's right,' Genista agreed, her heart sinking. She felt completely unequal to coping with a precocious fourteen-year-old with emotional problems.

'Marina will bring Lucy up here from her school. She's a nice kid, despite her upbringing. Sensible too, but she's at that age where they feel things intensely. I don't want her to grow up with the idea that there's no such thing as a happy marriage.'

'What are you trying to say?'

'That for the duration of Lucy's stay, you'll share my room. I've put your case in there. You can unpack while I make breakfast. I'm well aware that her visit gives you the perfect opportunity to get back at me, but I'm not asking for your co-operation for my sake—it's for hers. She worshipped her father, and she took it hard when he left.'

Genista touched her dry lips with the tip of her tongue. A wild idea had suddenly occurred to her.

'All right,' she agreed huskily. 'But there's one condition.'

Luke's eyes held hers.

'For as long as Lucy stays here I'll act the part of the deliriously happy new bride, but once she's gone, I want you to start divorce proceedings. You blackmailed me into this marriage, and if I have to I'll blackmail you into letting me out of it.'

'I see.'

It was impossible to judge his reactions from the even words. 'So. Now we both know where we stand. I owe Marina this much, I suppose. After all, I was the one who introduced Philip to Verity.'

A Verity who was now free, Genista reminded herself sickly. No wonder Luke wasn't raising any objections to her desire to be free!

'Very well, but if you cheat on me, our agreement will be rescinded, Genista.'

'I'll go and unpack my things.'

He was standing by the door, and she had to breathe in to squeeze past him. She could smell the clean fragrance of his cologne and for one mad moment she wanted to reach up and touch him, to press her body against him and feel his vital, compelling response.

'Mrs Meadows will be here soon. You might warn her about Lucy's impending arrival.' He walked towards her bed, twitching back the covers she had just disturbed. 'I don't want any gossip in the village,' he told her harshly. 'It might get to Lucy's ears.'

'I'll make the bed when I'm dressed.'

They were enemies. She could feel it in the silence which stretched between them, and she had to blink fiercely to prevent tears from forming.

It was shortly after four o'clock that the Citroën pulled up in front of the house in a spurt of gravel, disgorging an elegant dark-haired woman whom Genista would have recognised anywhere as Luke's sister, and a fair-haired teenager, still dressed in what was obviously her school uniform. She looked so vulnerable and young that Genista's heart went out to her. Had Marina told her daughter about her father's return?

'Luke, you wretch, how dare you get married without telling me? You do realise that you've robbed Lucy of her only chance of being a bridesmaid, don't you?' Marina called lightly as she walked into the house. Seen at closer quarters, she had a brittle quality, a nervous tension which communicated itself instantly to Genista. Despite her elegance, the older woman was nervous of Luke? She glanced covertly at her husband. He was frowning faintly, his attention focused not on Marina but on Lucy, who was hanging back slightly, her expression uncertain.

'Lucy would have hated being a bridesmaid,' he said decisively. 'How was school, little one?'

'Filthy!'

It was instantly obvious to Genista that uncle and niece shared a rapport which did not exist between mother and daughter. Physically they were not alike, until Lucy smiled, and then her wry expression bore a startling resemblance to her uncle's sardonic grimace.

'But she's looking forward to spending her half-term with you,' Marina interposed quickly, turning to Genista. 'Luke is a gem. Lucy often spends her half-terms with him. It's so convenient. Coming over to France means that she loses a day each way, and it just isn't worth it for the shorter breaks.'

Genista smiled politely, but secretly she felt a little surprised by Marina's attitude towards her child. It was scarcely maternal.

'I can't stay long, Luke,' she was saying quickly—too quickly, it seemed to Genista, as though she expected Luke to protest. 'Lucy, run upstairs and unpack. I want to speak to your uncle, and I have to leave right after dinner.'

'She's a teenager, not a child, Marina,' Luke said mildly when Lucy had gone. 'Have you told her about Philip?'

'I intended to, but as yet I haven't had the chance,' Marina began evasively.

'And as you plan to leave us right after dinner you won't have the opportunity to—right?' Luke enquired sardonically.

'Oh, Luke, it will come so much better from you,' Marina pleaded. 'I just can't tell her. My nerves . . .'

'You shouldn't have pumped her full of all that rubbish about Philip in the first place,' Luke said dryly, 'You're a fool, Marina.'

'That's a fine way to talk to your sister!' Marina

took umbrage instantly. 'It isn't often I ask you to help me, Luke. It's only a small thing, after all.'

'You think so?' If anything his voice was even drier. 'Leaving us with a sensitive teenager at the very start of our honeymoon, and expecting us to break the news to her that the father her mother has been reviling without cessation for the last four years is suddenly about to be welcomed back into the fold? I wonder if Philip really knows what he's letting himself in for?'

'That's a foul thing to say!' Marina's voice broke on the last word, and to Genista's dismay she saw tears in the older woman's eyes. 'I'm going up to my room.'

'There's no need to look at me as though I've just taken a starving child's crust,' Luke said curtly when his sister had gone. 'Marina isn't averse to turning on the tears if she thinks it will get her her own way.'

'She is your sister,' Genista pointed out mildly.

'I know, and that's one of the reasons I could never find it in my heart to really hate Philip. Poor devil!'

'He must love Marina if he's going back to her. Will you tell Lucy?'

'I expect I'll have to. Marina is quite capable of leaving without doing so and then calmly leaving Lucy to find out the truth for herself the next time she goes home. Marina was spoiled by our parents and as a result she seems to expect everyone to treat her indulgently. I hope Philip knows what he's doing.'

Suspecting that Marina was the type of woman who always changed for dinner, Genista went upstairs while Luke was busy in the library. They might have to share a room, but she was determined that they would spend as little time in it together as they could.

She was seated in front of the dressing table mirror applying her eye-shadow when she heard the faint tap on the door. She was wearing only a towelling wrap over her underclothes and she frowned, hesitating.

'It's Marina—may I come in?'

For a moment she felt deep disappointment. Had she been hoping it was Luke? He was hardly likely to knock on his own bedroom door. No doubt he was as anxious to avoid any intimacy with her as she was with him—although for completely different reasons. While she feared that his proximity might force her to betray her feelings for him, he felt only boredom for her sexual inexperience. He had expected to find in her a woman whose knowledge of lovemaking matched his own, and instead he had discovered that she knew next to nothing about the art of pleasing a man—apart from what he had taught her!

'Oh, I'm sorry, I didn't realise you weren't dressed,' Marina apologised. 'Where's Luke— downstairs?'

'He's in the library,' Genista told her. 'Did you want to talk to him?'

'Not unless he's in a far more accommodating mood than he was earlier,' Marina said frankly. 'I sometimes think he forgets that I'm five years older than he is. He's let his success as a businessman go to his head. All that nonsense about your being on your honeymoon!' She glanced covertly at Genista. 'We're both women of the world, my dear—I know my brother, and he's no monk. One only has to think of that bitch Verity to know that—he had a lucky escape there. She would have taken him for every penny he owned—and will still probably try, if I know her. Now that she no longer has Philip to batten on to, she's bound to try and get Luke under her thumb again. He doted on her, you know ...' She broke off as though realising that they were hardly sentiments likely to appeal to a newly married bride, adding hurriedly, 'But of course, Luke would never take her back. He's gone so hard—he would never forgive her. Now, as I was saying, all this foolishness about the pair of you being on your honeymoon. I'm sure you won't take it amiss when I say that where my brother is concerned, playing by the rules is not his forte, and nowadays ...'

'Everyone anticipates their marriage vows—is that what you were about to say?' Luke interposed smoothly, startling them both. 'Wrong, my dear sister. I didn't know Genista long enough beforehand to do so, even had she been willing. You're letting your cynicism cloud your judgement. As it happens, my wife was as pure and untouched as Lucy.'

From Marina's briefly assessing glance, Genista suspected that the other woman was surprised by Luke's revelations. She herself felt ready to die with embarrassment. How dared Luke discuss her like this!

'A virgin?' Marina's eyes rounded. 'I suppose I should have known. Nothing but the best for my brother—and certainly no second or third-hand goods! Verity wouldn't get a look in now, would she?'

'You're embarrassing Genista,' Luke said coolly, 'and insulting me. I married Genista for no other reason than that I love her.'

He was an excellent actor, Genista thought

bitterly. Marina stared at him in silence.

'And now, if you'll leave, I shall get changed for dinner, after which we shall discuss what is and is not to be said to Lucy.'

On the pretext of wanting to check the table, Genista left the bedroom shortly after Marina had gone. Luke was paused in the middle of unbuttoning his shirt and glanced at her sardonically.

'Running away?' he jeered. 'From what, I wonder? Me, or yourself?'

Genista found Lucy in the dining room. The girl had changed out of her uniform into a pretty cotton dress. She smiled rather hesitantly, reminding Genista once again of Luke.

'I'm sorry Mother has thrust me upon you like this,' she began apologetically. Her manner was adult, but the fingers twisting nervously together were not, and Genista smiled reassuringly.

'Nonsense! Luke loves having you here, I know that!'

Her lie was rewarded with a relieved smile.

'Mother is the end sometimes. She just doesn't think.' Lucy walked towards the window, her back hunched faintly defensively. 'I know all about her and Father getting together again. He writes to me, you see, although I haven't told her. It wasn't really disloyal. It's just that she gets in such a state about him. I was going to tell Uncle Luke about it, only with Father and Verity . . .'

'I'm sure he would have understood,' Genista soothed, feeling a sudden spurt of anger at the carelessness of adults. How could Lucy's parents have thrust such heavy burdens on her young shoulders? 'It's only right that you should care for your father as well as your mother. You must be pleased about the way things have turned out.'

'I want to be,' Lucy admitted, 'but I'm frightened—in case they part again,' she explained quickly. 'You see, mother is so . . . so volatile, and Father gets cross with her. I think that's why he left with Verity in the first place. I know it's wrong of me to say this, but it was she who enticed Father, and I'm not just saying that to defend him. She thought he had more money than Luke. You did know that she and Luke were engaged?' she asked hesitantly.

'Oh yes, I know all about that.' Whatever else happened Genista wouldn't add to Lucy's burdens. 'I suggest you wait for Luke to come downstairs, and then have a word with him. We can delay dinner for a few minutes. I think he'll be relieved to hear that you already know about your parents' reconciliation.'

'Mother was just going to leave me here for him to tell, was she? Poor Uncle Luke!'

Genista deliberately waylaid Marina when she came downstairs, and when Lucy disappeared in the direction of the library, returning ten minutes later with Luke, her face wreathed in smiles, Genista felt an involuntary pang of envy. How nice to be Lucy and know with complete confidence that whatever her problems she could take them to Luke in the sure knowledge that they would be solved.

She noticed, however, that Luke said nothing to his sister about Lucy's confidences, and judged that this was his way of punishing her for what she suspected he considered to be dereliction of her maternal duties. How would he punish her if he ever discovered she had been foolish enough to fall in love with him?

'Watch out for Verity, my dear,' Marina warned Genista in a low voice as they walked out to her car after dinner. 'I know Luke is in love with you, but Verity is a very determined woman—and an extremely beautiful one.'

In love with her! If only she knew, Genista thought miserably as the Citroën drove away. A chill little breeze played over her bare arms and she shivered slightly.

'You're cold. Better get back inside,' Luke said impersonally. 'I have some work to do, so I'll leave you and Lucy to get acquainted. I've promised her a shopping spree while she's here. It will give you both something to occupy yourselves with.'

'How very kind,' Genista said sarcastically. 'Is that the only way you know of satisfying a woman, Luke? Buying her things?'

He turned, and she shivered under the look in his eyes, but refused to let it daunt her. Lucy was waiting for them by the door, and she glanced quickly at them.

'Fancy a game of Scrabble?' Luke suggested.

She looked uncertainly from Luke to Genista and guessing what she was thinking Genista said gaily, 'I'd love it—how about you, Lucy?'

She told herself it wasn't because of what Luke had said about putting on a loving front; it was for Lucy, who had already been hurt enough by the adults in her life, and she made a vow that for the duration of Lucy's stay she would do everything in her power to preserve the façade of a happy marriage.

CHAPTER SEVEN

GENISTA opened her eyes slowly. She was lying on her side facing the window, sunshine pouring in through the curtains. She glanced at her watch. Half-past eight! She turned her head half fearfully, but she need not have worried—the other side of the bed, which had obviously been occupied by Luke, was now empty save for the impression of his head against the pillow and a faint rumpling of the sheet.

She had not heard him come to bed. The phone had rung just as she was on the point of going upstairs and he had disappeared into the library, much to her relief. Lucy was a sensitive and intelligent child, and she had no idea how she was going to manage to preserve the united front Luke was insisting on, in her presence. She pushed the bedclothes aside, tensing at the sudden nausea that overtook her. The meal the previous evening had been very rich, and it was no wonder she felt queasy—after all, she had eaten next to nothing over the last few days, being far too worked up to enjoy her food.

By the time she reached the bathroom the sickness had subsided, leaving her feeling faintly shaky and very relieved. Being ill was the last thing she could cope with at the moment. She sensed that Luke would have scant sympathy and look upon her 'symptoms' as a means of evading his instructions.

Lucy was just pouring herself a cup of coffee when Genista walked into the kitchen. Dressed in a tee-shirt and jeans, the girl looked even younger than she had done the evening before.

'Hi! I was just about to bring you a drink. Luke said not to wake you too early, and to tell you that he had to go to the office but that he'd be back around five.'

Subsiding thankfully into a chair, Genista took the cup of coffee Lucy was proffering. At least she would have one day without Luke's unkind taunts and control-draining presence.

'I thought I might go riding this morning,' Lucy informed her over breakfast. 'There's a stable just down the road. Fancy coming with me?'

Outside the sun shone mellowly on the immaculate gardens, and the prospect of being out of doors was very tempting.

'I'd love to,' Genista admitted. 'But I'm not a very good rider—in fact I haven't been on horseback since my teens, and I haven't had time to explore the gardens yet.'

'How about a compromise, then?' Lucy suggested cheerfully. 'Riding this morning, lunch here and then an exploration of the gardens—they stretch for quite a way, you know. As well as the formal gardens round the house, there are a couple of acres of grounds with woods, and a very pretty lake.'

Lucy voiced no curiosity that Genista should know so little of her new home, and Genista silently blessed the girl's ready acceptance. She seemed happier this morning, and while Genista tidied away their breakfast things and wrote a note for Mrs Meadows Lucy dashed upstairs to change into riding gear. It would be perfectly all right for her to wear jeans, she had assured Genista when she expressed her doubts, and they would be able to hire hats from the stables.

It had been so long since Genista visited the country proper that she had forgotten the simple delight of walking down a country lane early in the morning. The sky was that particularly soft shade of blue only seen in June, dew still sparkling on the grassy verges of the road. Beyond the hedge crops gleamed golden in fields speckled with the silky scarlet of poppies.

'Umm, just taste this air!' Lucy sighed blissfully. 'It's like breathing freedom! I really hate school. Mother was very clever. She should have gone on to Cambridge, but she met Father instead. She keeps going on to me about having a career. She can't seem to understand that the things that interest her don't appeal to me.'

'What would you like to do?' Genista asked, sympathising, but knowing how radically one's views could change between fourteen and twenty-four. In ten years' time Lucy might bitterly regret not being able to support herself. Genista had found that even where money was not an issue, many girls of her own generation found their careers so stimulating that they did not want to give them up. Thinking back to her own teens and the years before she met Richard, Genista could well remember viewing unmarried girls in the village in their early twenties with mixed pity and horror, and she suspected that modern teenagers were no different, although with the example of her parents' marriage before her, Lucy was bound to be a little more mature.

The stables were in a small hollow a little over a mile from the house. They had recently changed hands, Genista learned from the cheerful girl they found in the office-cum-tack room, but she was sure that Mr Lawson would be able to fix them up with a couple of mounts, if they could wait fifteen minutes until he had finished the lesson he was giving.

With the whole day stretching lazily ahead of them, Genista was quite content to sit down and watch the stable cat basking drowsily in a sheltered corner of the yard, while Lucy and the stablegirl chattered happily together.

She hadn't realised the intensity of the strain she had been under since her marriage, until she felt tiredness sweep over her. The fresh air probably hadn't helped she acknowledged, stifling a yawn. Heavens, she couldn't go to sleep here! Nevertheless that was what she was on the point of doing when a pleasant male voice roused her.

'Sleeping Beauty, I presume,' its owner teased. 'What a pity you woke up. I was looking forward to rousing you in the time-honoured fashion.'

From her sitting position on the old chair she had been provided with, Genista had to look up a long way to reach the thin, tanned face and amused blue eyes of the man who had just walked into the yard. As he was dressed casually in an open-necked shirt and jeans and ancient riding boots, scuffed and worn, she had no difficulty in placing him as the owner of the stables.

He was younger than she had expected—some-where in his late twenties, she guessed, and to judge by the way he was looking at her slender figure in her old, tight-fitting jeans, horses weren't his only interest.

'I'm Trevor Lawson,' he said, introducing him-self. 'Belinda said you were interested in hiring a couple of mounts.'

'Yes, that's right,' Genista agreed, scrambling to her feet, aware of the warm tinge to her skin, where his eyes had rested on it—and knowing he was aware of it too.

'My husband's niece was keen to ride and I said I'd come with her, although I'm no expert.'

'Husband? So you're married?' Did he really sound faintly regretful, or was she merely imagining it? 'Well, if you'd just care to follow me back into the office, to register, I'll see what I can do. I've only taken over this business recently, although I've lived in the area for several years.' He walked with a slight limp, which Genista hadn't noticed at first, and as though aware of it, he patted his leg lightly and said, 'I got this through T.T. racing—I was lucky I didn't lose my leg. My doctor recommended that I take up riding for therapy. I enjoyed it so much that I bought this place. No one wants a motor-cycle rider who's afraid of falling off, and although I'm virtually okay now, as far as track racing goes, I've lost my nerve.'

Although she was surprised that he should confide so much in someone who was virtually a stranger, Genista smiled sympathetically.

'Do you live locally?' Trevor asked her, over his shoulder as he walked into the 'office'.

'Not far away,' Genista replied, filling in the form he gave her. He looked at what she had written and whistled silently. 'You're married to Luke?'

He sounded so surprised that Genista flushed defensively.

'Oh, I'm sorry,' Trevor apologised instantly. 'I didn't mean it that way. It's just that I know Luke fairly well and he never mentioned . . . that is. . . .'

'They fell in love and were married almost straight away.' Lucy told him, materialising beside them. 'I think it's jolly romantic!'

They exchanged smiles over her head at the schoolgirlish slang. Oh, to be Lucy's age again, Genista thought silently, when life could be viewed so easily at face value.

'Well, I think I'd better give you a fairly placid mount for your first day out,' Trevor was saying. 'I don't want Luke accusing me of not taking proper care of you. He helped me a good deal with the finance for this venture,' he added to Genista when Lucy had been taken away by Belinda to choose her mount. 'A lot of people tend to think of him as a bit of an ogre—his reputation as a big businessman, I suppose. It gives the impression of ruthlessness, but of course Luke isn't like that at all. He's been marvellous to me, and the only condition he's made is that I teach the kids from the local handicapped school to ride, twice a week— something which is a pleasure anyway. To see the way those kids enjoy themselves, the freedom riding brings them . . .'

He talked about his work with the children while he harnessed the gentle mare he had chosen for Genista. She was still trying to come to terms with Luke in this new role as benefactor!

'Of course, Luke hates anyone talking about his generosity,' Trevor added as he helped her into the saddle. 'But then I suppose you already know that. He's a very complex character. I should hate to get on the wrong side of him, although one feels that he would always be scrupulously fair, unless of course his emotions were involved.' He looked thoughtfully at Genista, now seated on the back of the pretty bay mare. 'They say that still waters run deep and I imagine Luke's run deeper than most, but then you look as though you have the courage to cope with anything life might hold for you.'

Had she? Genista mused as she and Lucy cantered past a herd of chomping cows. It was something she had never given much thought to in the past. She would need a great deal of courage if she was to survive her time with Luke and emerge unscathed from the agony their eventual parting would cause her.

It was lunchtime before she and Lucy returned to the house. Mrs Meadows had left a cold meal for them, and over it, Lucy giggled that she rather suspected Trevor had fancied Genista.

'I suspect he's the same with all women,' Genista told her dryly. 'He's certainly something of a charmer.'

'Umm—I think Belinda's in love with him,' Lucy told her, surprising Genista with her perception. 'She looks at him the same way Uncle Luke looks at you—sort of hungry.'

Genista could have told her that there was more than one type of hunger, but she had no wish to disillusion her. Instead she reminded her that she had promised to show her round the gardens. She had no idea what Luke normally did in the evening. There was a huge freezer in the kitchen and preparing dinner would be no problem. She removed some steak, deciding that steak and salad with pâté for a first course, and fresh fruit afterwards, was the sort of thing that appealed to most tastes.

They walked round the formal gardens first. Half way round Genista suddenly felt very dizzy and had to sit down on the wooden bench conveniently to hand. The dizziness was followed by a bout of the same nausea she had experienced that morning, and she began to wonder if she could possibly have eaten something that disagreed with her.

Lucy watched her anxiously for a few minutes, but when she asked if Genista would prefer to go back to the house Genista shook her head.

If she went up to her room she would only lie there thinking about Luke, imagining how it could have been had he cared for her; had he felt love for her and not merely lust. The mere thought of his lovemaking made her tremble inwardly. Whatever happened she must never again allow herself to be trapped in a situation where she was so vulnerable to him. He had told her he was marrying her to satiate his desire, but that had been before; before he knew how inexperienced she was, and now that desire seemed to have waned completely, and he must surely be regretting their marriage. By the time they had reached the lake Genista was quite convinced that had it not been for his pride and the fact that Lucy was visiting them, he would have suggested they apply for a divorce the moment they returned from Cumbria. After all, despite his earlier comments he had made no attempt to so much as touch her since their return.

Telling herself that she ought to be feeling relief, not an emotion which was perilously close to disappointment, she allowed Lucy to point out to her an old-fashioned punt secured by a small landing stage.

'I wanted to try it last year, but Luke says he doesn't think it would be safe. He wants to drain the lake and have it cleaned. He says it's feet deep in mud, and that the punt could quite easily sink.'

Looking into the still, murky water, Genista was inclined to agree with him, although like Lucy she could not quite ignore the age-old appeal of studying the bracken depths looking for some signs of life.

'Luke wants to stock it with koi carp,' Lucy told her. 'They get so tame that you can feed them by hand.'

'I know,' Genista agreed, remembering a holiday in Italy at a villa where one of the highlights of her day had been feeding the beautifully coloured carp in their marble pool.

'Do you think my parents will stay together this time?' Lucy asked abruptly.

'I don't know, Lucy.' Genista tried to be as gentle as she could. 'Life doesn't come with guarantees, although I know that's sometimes hard to accept. Try to tell yourself that it's enough that they care sufficiently for one another to *try* again. I think they're both very brave.'

'Or foolish,' Lucy suggested in a slightly muffled voice. 'Genista, how do you know when love is real?'

'It's something I can't explain.' It was getting towards late afternoon, and Genista knew that she should suggest that they return to the house, but it had obviously cost Lucy a great deal to confide in her, and she couldn't turn her away without at least trying to reassure her. 'First you have to try and differentiate between "real" and "for ever." When we fall in love, we take it for granted that that love will last for ever—sometimes it doesn't. That doesn't mean that we've failed, or that it's someone's fault. Life and people can't remain static all the time; things change. One of the hardest things for anyone to learn is the acceptance that happiness doesn't always last for ever.'

'But knowing that, how can anyone commit their

lives to another person?' The anguish in Lucy's eyes struck a chord deep within her own heart. How indeed? she could have said, but instead she reached for Lucy's hand, tanned, and faintly grubby, but already showing signs of the beauty the girl would one day possess.

'Quite easily. I can't find the words to explain to you how it happens Lucy. I do understand how you feel; when I was not very much older than you something happened to me that made me feel as though I could never trust anyone else again as long as I lived—and certainly never love them.' Engrossed in trying to reassure Lucy, Genista didn't hear the faint sounds betraying the fact that they were no longer alone. 'But I did, and when you love you're willing to risk all the uncertainties in the world. That's something which is inherent in every human being. You wait and see. Love, true, proper love, does cast out all fear, which is what we're talking about, isn't it? The fear of something going wrong; of being hurt. When I fell in love with ...' A twig snapped underfoot, and Genista spun round. Luke was leaning against a tree trunk several yards away. His face had gone white.

'Uncle Luke!' Lucy raced towards him and the look of bitter hatred Genista had seen in his eyes was banished instantly.

Lucy chattered ceaselessly to him all the way back to the house, pausing only to draw breath.

'We went riding this morning,' she confided. 'I think Mr Lawson really fancied Genista. He couldn't stop looking at her, could he?'

She turned to Genista for corroboration. Although the path was broad enough for three, she had fallen back, unable to bear such close proximity to Luke.

'I've already told you,' Genista replied lightly, 'I suspect he flirts a little with all his lady customers. I wasn't sure what to do about dinner,' she told Luke. 'I've prepared a salad and I thought we'd have steak with it . . .'

'Have whatever you like,' Luke told her curtly. 'I'm dining out.'

Lucy pulled a face, but he wouldn't be swayed. He went upstairs when they entered the house, and Genista dawdled in the kitchen, not wanting to go into the bedroom while he was still there.

Lucy wanted to watch a particular television programme and she had gone up to her bedroom to do so when Genista heard the kitchen door open. Luke was dressed elegantly in soft suede cream pants and a dark blue silk shirt, a leather jacket in his hand. His clothes, although expensive, were not the sort Genista would have expected him to wear for a business meeting, and jealousy tore at her with red-hot claws as she envisaged the sort of surroundings for which such casual clothes might be worn—a nightclub perhaps; a fashionable restaurant, but with whom? Her mouth tightened. So much for Luke's instructions that Lucy was not to be allowed to suspect how things were between them! A hundred angry words clamoured for utterance, but all she could say was, 'Is this how you expect to convince Lucy that we're in love? By going out and leaving us alone?'

'She'd be far more disillusioned if I stayed,' Luke said harshly. 'Because the way I feel at the moment, I'm liable to throttle you. And don't bother to wait up for me.'

The phone rang as the Maserati roared down the drive, and Genista answered it. A woman with a smokily seductive voice asked for Luke and when

Genista said that he had gone out, she laughed softly.

'Good. I thought he might be late, but he's remembered that I hate to be kept waiting.'

Genista could barely touch the steak. Images of Luke dining in some candlelit restaurant with the owner of the huskily wanton voice tormented her. She would not be a naïve virgin! She would know everything there was to know about pleasing a man, it had all been there in her voice.'

After dinner they would dance, perhaps, Luke holding her close enough to his body for her to feel every sinuous movement, and then later. . . .

'Genista! Are you all right?'

Lucy's concerned voice brought her abruptly back to the dining table, and the mutilated roll lying in pieces on her plate.

'I'm fine.' Only she wasn't. Her legs felt dreadfully weak, and silly tears weren't far away.

'Well, I think it's really mean of Uncle Luke to work tonight.'

'I expect it was something unavoidable,' Genista said lightly, trying not to let her voice tremble. She pushed away her strawberries and cream untouched. 'If you don't mind, Lucy, I think I'll have an early night. I'm feeling dreadfully tired for some reason. It must be all that fresh air.'

'Mm, I'm feeling quite sleepy myself. I want to write to Mother, so I'll have an early night as well. Shall I do the washing up for you?'

There was a luxurious dishwasher in the kitchen, but nevertheless they did the washing up between them, Genista finding comfort in the mechanically routine task. Lucy chatted about her school as they worked, and Genista learned that despite the younger girl's averred dislike of school, in reality she had a keen interest in literature and the arts.

'Have you ever thought of becoming a librarian?'
Genista suggested, when Lucy was bemoaning the
lack of opportunities for people with an arts
degree. 'And it needn't be merely library work,
although that in itself is a very good career.
Television and radio stations often need re-
searchers; if your qualifications are good enough
you could get a super job.'

It was something which Lucy had obviously not
thought of previously, and by the time they had
exhausted the subject it was later than Genista had
realised.

She tried to soak away some of her tension in a
hot bath, secure in the knowledge that Luke was
hardly likely to leave his companion at ten-thirty
to come rushing back to his unwanted wife!

She scented the water generously with her
favourite bath oil and lay back, trying to force her
tense muscles to relax.

Afterwards she wrapped herself in a huge fluffy
peach towel and started to dry her hair.

The bedroom she shared with Luke was obviously the master bedroom.

In addition to the bedroom itself, there was a
bathroom, luxuriously equipped and tiled with
toning sanitary ware in shades of coffee and brown.
The bath was huge, and set into the floor—more
than adequate for two people, Genista had reflected, before she realised the direction her unwary
thoughts were taking.

Off the bedroom was a dressing room lined with
fitted wardrobes, all mirror-fronted. Luke had indicated that she was to make use of them, and she
had hung her few clothes in one small corner. She
would need to make a trip to London to collect

the rest of her things. Luke had barely given her time on their brief call on the way back from Cumbria. She also wanted to collect her car.

Her hair lay over her shoulders in a cascade of russet silk. The bedroom was decorated in shades of toning peach and coffee; neither too masculine nor fluffily feminine. Genista loved the pure cotton sheets and beautiful handmade bedspread. The sheets felt blissfully cool as she slid beneath them. She heard the grandfather clock in the hall strike eleven as she closed her eyes.

Genista opened her eyes. The bedroom was all in darkness, and at first she couldn't place the sound that had woken her. Outside she heard an owl and shivered, shrinking back against the pillows as a shadow detached itself from the wall.

'Luke!'

'Who did you think it was?' he drawled unkindly. 'Bob? or Trevor Lawson?'

She had no defence against him in this mood. He stood silhouetted by the window, his body powerfully lithe in the hip hugging cream pants, his shirt unfastened, as he started to remove it.

'Aren't you going to ask me if I enjoyed my evening?'

His goading touched a painful nerve. She sat up in bed, unaware of the purity of her features in the moonlight, her hair spread round her like a soft cloak.

'I didn't realise wifely concern was supposed to be part of our bargain. What do you want me to do? Ask how much you enjoyed making love to another woman? Marriage to me was an expensive price to pay for satisfying your lust, Luke, especially now that you no longer want me.'

'What makes you think that?' His tone was softly

jeering. 'And as for being satisfied . . .'

Her heart seemed to have lodged in the back of her throat. She made a small sound of protest, muffled beneath the hands which lifted her from the bed, removing her thin cotton covering to reveal every slender contour of her quivering flesh.

'Some appetites are fed by starvation,' Luke said slowly, his eyes beginning a slow inspection of the moonlit flesh beneath his hands. 'And others thrive on feeding.'

Meaning, no doubt, that his desire for her was in no way diminished by having spent the last few hours in someone else's arms, Genista thought, trying to quell her growing feeling of nausea. She wouldn't let him make love to her merely to satisfy a need!

She started to tell him so, fear silencing her as she saw savage hunger in his eyes. Perhaps his evening had not been as successful as she had imagined. Perhaps his girl-friend had deliberately led him on, teasing and enticing but withholding herself, and she was merely being used as a vehicle to slake his thirst for someone else. She thought she had experienced every pain it was possible for a human being to experience, but now she knew that this was not so. The thought that Luke was contemplating making love for her purely for physical release brought an agony that made her feel physically ill.

'I'm tired, Luke . . .' She couldn't bring herself to look at him as she uttered the lie, but she hoped it would have the desired effect and that he would release her. His thumbs were stroking the inner flesh of her wrists seductively, and she wanted nothing so much as to melt passionately against him, feeling him stir with the same primitive force which was already weakening her resistance.

'Tired? Can't you think of a better excuse than that?'

'All right then, I don't want you,' Genista lied desperately. 'I hate you touching me, Luke. I wish you'd go away and leave me alone . . .'

'Oh, I shall,' he said softly through gritted teeth, 'but not until I've made you beg and plead for me to stay with you, Genista. Before tonight's over that cool, frosty little voice of yours will be sobbing my name, ragged with passion—A passion I already know you can experience.'

His own voice had taken on a deeper timbre which found an answering chord deep inside her. She longed to refute his words, but her tongue seemed to cleave to the roof of her mouth, preventing speech whilst an intense longing pulsated within her. In the moon-shadowed room she could see Luke's dark outline; the tanned flesh of his chest, rising lightly with his breathing, the lean tautness of his hips, the powerful muscles of his thighs, roughened with their light covering of dark hair beneath his cream pants. He came towards her and she retreated instinctively, until she was pressing herself back against the bed, her body tensing as she waited for him to touch her. His hands either side of her head on the pillow imprisoned her, his lean body only inches away, as he lowered his head and touched her lips almost experimentally.

She tried to avoid the caress, twisting her head frantically away, but each time she did so her cheek brushed the hard warmth of his hands, while her own were held rigidly at her sides for fear they might inadvertently come into contact with Luke's body.

His lips moved from her mouth to her cheek.

She turned away desperately, realising her mistake when her lips immediately came into contact with Luke's. He made no attempt to hurry the kiss, taking his time, forcing her lips to part for him, and still he made no other attempt to touch her. She tensed in anticipation of the sensual demand implicit in the intimacy of his kiss, but it never came, instead just when all her own yearning desire rose up inside her to overcome the barriers of her self-control, her lips were released, their hunger unappeased, the briefly tantalising kisses pressed lightly on her face no compensation for the abrupt cessation of the drugging pressure of his mouth on hers.

Genista endured the torment as long as she could, willing herself not to humiliate herself any further by allowing him to see how much he had already aroused her. If she just forced herself to endure his deliberate arousal a little while longer he was sure to grow bored with the game and release her. But she was soon forced to confess that his control was the greater, as minute succeeded long, agonising minute and every part of her body was urging her to bury her fingers in the thick dark hair growing low on the nape of his neck, and unashamedly hold his mouth against hers to complete that kiss he had broken off so cruelly.

Her body ached for his touch. She had to close her eyes against the sudden intruding recollection of his tanned fingers cupping the creamy softness of her breast, stroking it into urgent fullness, before moving downwards, coaxing from her unawakened body the responses which had eventually driven her into his arms in a frenzy of need.

It wouldn't be that way this time, she told herself. She mustn't allow it to be that way, but as his

breath warmed her throat and her body traitor-
ously remembered all she had willed it to forget, a
soft, husky sound broke past her closed lips.

She stilled the soft whimper immediately, but not
before Luke had heard it.

'It's not quite as easy as you thought, is it,
Genista?' he taunted softly. 'It's hard to be high
and mighty when your body is crying out for satisfaction, isn't it? Well, now you know how I felt.
Did you think I enjoyed it?' he demanded savagely,
'Do you think any man enjoys wanting a woman
the way I wanted you?'

'Wanting without loving is ... degrading!'
Genista flung at him, close to tears.

'Do you think I don't know that? But that
doesn't mean it isn't possible, so come down off
your cloud and acknowledge that you're a human
being, just like any other.'

She told herself that he just wanted to humiliate
her; just wanted some sort of warped revenge because he resented having wanted her, but when he
pinned her wildly thrashing hands behind her back
and let his lips wander at will over the pale silkiness
of her body, she was soon far beyond caring. His
lightest touch seemed to ignite fires she had never
dreamed could burn; reveal a sensuality she had
never known she possessed, and while her mind
writhed in humiliated agony at the punishment he
was deliberately inflicting her body responded with
an intensity which seemed to feed his deep hunger.

His name rose sobbingly to her lips, cried wren-
chingly through mingled pleasure and pain, and
although she glimpsed satisfaction in his eyes as he
raised his head to acknowledge his victory, the hard
pressure of his hands was not withdrawn, the torment continuing until she could bear her self-

imposed restraints no longer and her fingers
trembled in anguish against his skin, their mutual
passion blazing up into an inferno which carried
them both over the edge of the earth to a place
where nothing mattered but the dousing of its
flames.

'Please, Luke!' Genista murmured weakly at one
point when the withholding of his ultimate possession was an agony she could no longer endure.

Salty tears poured down her cheeks, her pride
was in tatters, but she no longer cared. All she
wanted was the pleasure of Luke's complete possession. His skin tasted of salt and sweat, and she
touched it with a hunger which she could no longer
hide, shaking with the depth of her need, pleading
mutely for the final act which would turn them
from two separate human beings into one complete
entity. His arms slid round her, holding her against
him, his breathing harshly ragged. She could feel
the hard pressure of his desire, and melted on a
soundless moan beneath the fierce pressure of a
kiss which drove back the final barriers, as at last
he answered the unspoken plea of her body.

She knew with some inner instinct she had not
known she possessed that for him this was the first
time he had *fully* possessed her without holding
back, and tinging her despair that she had given
way so easily to the seduction of her senses was
triumph that for a few brief seconds at least he had
wanted her every bit as desperately as she had
wanted him.

Later, when she was on the verge of sleep, he
leaned over her, cupping her face, so that he could
watch her eyes.

'Never tell me again that you don't want me,' he
told her cruelly. 'Please, Luke . . .' The savage

mimicry of her pleas to him made her blench.
'Perhaps I should have recorded it, just to remind
myself of what you're like when you're a woman. I
could have played it to Bob, and let him know
what he's missing.'

Nothing had changed, Genista thought, as the
tears rolled silently down her cheeks, and she had
been a fool to think it might just be because they
had shared a few ecstatic seconds of pleasure. For
her, what she had given to Luke had been given
with love, but he had taken with revenge and lust,
and that was something she must always remember.

CHAPTER EIGHT

SHE was alone again when she woke up, so much
so that she might have doubted that the elemental
lovemaking of the previous evening had ever taken
place had it not been for the faint bruises on her
arms, and the memory of how her body had responded with pagan abandon to Luke's mastery.

She and Lucy went to London after an early
lunch. Lucy was enchanted with the teenage
fashions in the shops, and Genista watched her
indulgently, knowing that despite her outer care-
free air inwardly her thoughts were on her parents.

They had afternoon tea at Fortnum's—a treat
which very much appealed, if Lucy's wide-eyed
appreciation was anything to go by—and afterwards they went back to Genista's apartment.

'You did get married in a rush, didn't you?' Lucy
commented as Genista opened her wardrobe door.

'What a gorgeous fur!' she exclaimed enviously, spotting Genista's fox jacket. 'I wouldn't have left that behind.'

'I don't normally have much use for it in June,' Genista told her dryly. Seeing her winter clothes hanging in the cupboard reminded her painfully that by winter she could very well be back in this apartment—alone. Only she knew how close she had come last night to breathing her love—only she knew that she had betrayed it. Every kiss, every caress had been an open admission of her feelings, but Luke did not know it. No doubt he was accustomed to women who treated sex in much the same way as a man—as an appetite to be indulged and then forgotten, whereas for her the act of love had been a culmination of all that she felt for him.

The cream cake she had consumed at Fortnum's at Lucy's instigation sat rather heavily on her stomach. She had felt queasy on waking again as well, she remembered uneasily—then a sudden horrified dread almost toppled her into the nearest chair.

'Are you all right, Genista?' Lucy questioned worriedly. 'You don't look well at all.'

'Oh, it's nothing,' Genista was quick to reassure her. 'I just felt a little bit queasy—that cream cake, I think.'

If only she could believe that that was true! It seemed impossible that the dread lying at the back of her mind could turn into reality, but on the drive back to the house it kept returning, surfacing with increasing frequency despite her determined efforts to ignore it. She was being silly, she told herself more than once, and besides, surely it was far too soon . . . She knew so little about these things. She counted backwards slowly, her hands clenching suddenly on the driving wheel, as she realised what the events of the last few days had made her forget. She was probably imagining things, she told herself over and over again. Emotional crises often had disturbing effects upon the body. There was nothing to worry about; no point in raising spectres. Even so, by the time she was turning into the drive she was feverishly tense, and it was left to Lucy to point out the elegant BMW parked outside.

'Visitors!' she exclaimed. 'Uncle Luke must be back.'

Luke had left that morning without giving Genista any clue as to when she might expect him back, and she had wondered with a pang if he intended to see the owner of the seductively husky voice. She got out of her car shakily, her mind still on the frightening possibility that she might actually be carrying his child.

The moment she entered the hall she was aware of an alien presence; it wasn't just the smell of Opium hanging heavily on the air, or the way the library door had been left open, it was an actual physical awareness, like goosebumps.

'Darling, at last! I thought you were never coming!'

She recognised the husky, feminine voice before its owner walked languidly into the hall, her lips parting on a small 'oh' of tribute to the other woman's beauty.

She was dark-haired, tall, with the fluid elegance of a model, beautifully dressed and made up, and several years older than Genista. A huge diamond, large enough to be 'showy', glittered on her right hand, and her nails were painted a vivid dark red.

'Oh!' She paused when she saw Genista, eyeing her disdainfully. 'The child bride, I presume. Luke really did make a mistake this time, didn't he? Where is he by the way?—he promised to meet me here at six. We're supposed to be going out to dinner.'

Her sangfroid took Genista's breath away. Lucy was standing behind her, and as Genista turned she caught the look of bitter hatred on the girl's face.

'What are you doing here?' she stormed furiously. 'You broke up my parents' marriage and now you want to spoil things for Genista! Well, Uncle Luke doesn't want you back. He knows exactly what you are. You might have fooled him once, but . . .'

'That's enough, Lucy,' Genista interposed gently, seeing that she was close to breaking down completely. It was as though she had known the identity of the visitor all along, and refused to acknowledge it. Even last night when she answered the phone the knowledge had been there. So this was Verity, the woman her husband had loved. And still did? Was that why he had made love to *her* with such savage intensity? Because of this woman!

This time her nausea couldn't be quelled. She was violently sick in the cloakroom, adding further to her sense of humiliation. When she emerged, pale and shaken, Verity eyed her superciliously.

'How very dramatic,' she murmured acidly. 'Haven't you learned yet, you silly little girl, that Luke abhors emotionalism?'

Lucy had gone—to her room, Genista presumed. How did one entertain one's husband's ex-mistress and possibly future wife? It was not something she was ever likely to find in a book of etiquette.

'There's no way you can keep him, you know,'

Verity continued. 'Oh, I've no doubt that he doesn't want to hurt you. In fact, if you behave sensibly now you could come out of it quite pleasantly—finance-wise.'

'But without Luke,' Genista said, surprised at her own ability to remain so calm when inwardly she felt as though she were being torn to pieces.

'Oh, without Luke, of course,' Verity agreed softly. 'But then you can hardly have expected to keep him; a mere child like you.' She moved sinuously, revealing the perfect curves of her body, her expression almost felinely triumphant. 'You see, my dear, compared with me you can only be the clumsiest amateur. I'm sure we don't need to fence with one another. Luke is a deeply sexual man, and I know how to arouse, fan and appease that sexuality as no other woman ever will. It is true that I stupidly allowed a natural need for security to blind me to the truth, but fortunately I realised in time that Luke is the man for me, just as I am the only woman for him. Oh, he may have amused himself with you; enjoyed the novelty of making love to a complete novice, but you could never hope to keep him satisfied for long.'

Her words only echoed Genista's own fears and feelings. It was obvious that Luke had confided in Verity; had told her about their marriage, and she did not know which was the hardest to bear—the knowledge that he had openly discussed her with Verity, or the fact that much of what Verity was saying was true. The mere fact that Luke had invited his old love to the house, where Lucy would see her, shrieked the truth out loud; his need for her was so great that even Lucy's feelings no longer mattered.

She still had some tattered remnants of dignity,

some age-old instinct which made her lift her head
and say proudly,

'If Luke wants me to leave he only has to tell
me. I have no intention of staying where I'm not
wanted, but until he does, this is still my home,
and you are still an intruder. Coming here when
you must have known that Lucy would be here is
in the worst possible taste, in view of the fact that
you were living with her father until quite recently.
As you say, we have no need to fence with one
another, so I'm sure *you'll* understand *me* when I
tell you that I'm going upstairs to Lucy, leaving
you to wait for my husband on your own.'

'Your husband!' Verity laughed mockingly.
'How the words trip off your tongue, but very soon
they'll only be an empty phrase. Luke is mine!'

The words reverberated through Genista's mind
as she hurried upstairs. As she had expected she
found Lucy huddled up on her bed, her expression
woeful.

'She said Uncle Luke had asked her to come
here!' she burst out as Genista opened the door. 'I
don't believe it. He wouldn't do a thing like that—
he hates her!'

'I'm sure whatever he did was for a good reason,'
Genista soothed. After all, it was the truth. No
doubt to Luke his love for Verity was an adequate
reason for putting it before everything else. 'Look,'
she suggested, 'why don't you give your mother
and father a ring? I'm sure they'll be delighted to
hear from you. They weren't planning to go away,
were they?'

Lucy shook her head, and Genista could see that
her suggestion had taken root. They made the call
together, Lucy insisting that Genista stay while she
spoke to both her parents.

'Father wants me to go home,' she told Genista as she replaced the receiver. 'Oh, Genista, they both sounded so happy! Mother was quite different, more like she used to be before . . . before . . .'

'You'll have to speak to your uncle before you make any plans to go to France,' Genista warned her. When Lucy was on the phone she had heard a car outside and automatically her body tensed in dread of the confrontation to come. Verity must have made her presence known to Luke by now. Was she in his arms? Was he assuring her that she, Genista, would be leaving his house at the earliest possible opportunity. The child he had given her was destined never to know its father. She tried not to let the thought hurt.

She was in their room when Luke walked in. He threw his jacket down on to the bed, and loosened his tie impatiently.

'Verity tells me you were very unpleasant to her. Why?' he demanded without preamble. 'She is a guest in my house and as such entitled to courtesy if nothing else.'

'While I, as your wife, am entitled to nothing, I suppose,' Genista challenged. 'Have you any idea of the effect it had on Lucy to find her here?'

Just for a moment an expression she could not fathom crossed his face, but it was gone before she could begin to unravel it.

'Don't hide behind Lucy, Genista,' he said harshly. 'You insulted Verity, and I should like to know why.'

'Insulted her? On the contrary!' Genista took a deep breath and held it. Whatever she said about his mistress Luke would side with Verity. Arguing with him was pointless. It only caused her more pain.

'I'm the one who's been insulted, Luke,' she said quietly at last. 'Insulted by being forced to endure sex without love; a marriage which makes a mockery of all that marriage should be.'

She heard the door slam, but it was several minutes before she was able to turn round—minutes during which she had battled against the tears threatening to fall, but it was all in vain. She was alone in the room, and several minutes later she heard the hum of the BMW's engine and saw the two people sitting in the car.

Lucy was slightly subdued over dinner, and Genista hoped she had not heard them quarrelling. She thought that given time Lucy would come to realise that men and women could find happiness together if they had enough love and trust, but she sensed that the younger girl was hurt by Luke's behaviour.

'Are you going to wait up for Uncle Luke?' she asked Genista anxiously after dinner.

Genista shook her head, striving to show a confidence she could not feel. She had no wish to destroy Luke's relationship with his niece, although she suspected that Verity would soon make sure there was room only for herself in his life.

When she did go to bed she lay sleepless, waiting for his return. Dawn was breaking before she acknowledged that he would not be back—not that night, at least. The anguish was almost unbearable.

She managed to put on a brave face in front of Lucy, letting the younger girl think that Luke had returned and gone out again, and hoping that Lucy would not think to comment on the fact that his car was still outside.

She had been sick again, and could now ignore

the signs no longer. She was carrying Luke's child. A part of her paganly rejoiced in the knowledge while another, more sensible part pointed out the problems she would have to face as a single parent, and the possible effect the lack of a father could have on her child. It was still too early to think about visiting her doctor, but intuitively she knew that she had conceived Luke's baby.

Lucy had decided to go riding again, but this time Genista declined to accompany her. Hadn't she once read somewhere that the early weeks could be critical for an unborn child? The very fact that she was so anxious about the safety of the life she carried told her how precious it had already become to her in such a short space of time.

She was sitting in the garden, trying to concentrate on a book she had found in the library when she heard footsteps on the gravel path. At first she thought it was Luke, and her heart leapt in anticipation, but it was Bob's more homely features which she saw when she looked upwards.

'Luke not here?' he asked her, frowning when she shook her head. 'He rang me last night and asked me to bring some papers down here. He said they were urgent.'

'I've no idea where he is,' Genista admitted. 'Can you stay and have lunch with me, or do you have to rush back?'

'Oh, I think I could manage to endure lunch with a beautiful woman,' Bob said with a grin. 'You're looking pale, Gen, is everything all right?'

'Can you think of one good reason why it shouldn't be?' Genista parried. 'Come inside with me, I'll fix us some lunch and you can tell me all about Elaine.'

'She's doing fine—much better than the doctor

thought at first. She's being so incredibly brave—you've no idea. I never dreamed she had so much inner strength. There was a time when I thought she would simply give up and die, but she's fighting with everything she's got.'

'I'm glad,' Genista said simply. 'But she's got a lot to fight for, Bob. A husband, her child . . .'

'Hey, do I detect a certain . . . unhappiness? Forgive me for prying, Gen, but to be honest I was surprised when you married Luke out of the blue like that. Don't get me wrong—I'm not surprised he fell so heavily for you, but you've never been a girl to act rashly. I might seem a middle-aged old fuddy-duddy, but I assure you I haven't forgotten the power of sexual attraction or the havoc it can wreak if it's mistaken for love.'

'There was no mistake. The trouble was that I didn't realise how much I loved him until it was too late. Oh, Bob!' Once the tears started to come she couldn't stem them. He took her in his arms awkwardly, proffering a large comforting handkerchief, and patting her gently on the back.

'What's the matter, Gen? Do you want to talk about it?'

'Luke doesn't love me.' The relief of saying it was only momentary. 'He never loved me, Bob, he just wanted me.' She tried to explain what had happened, between sobs, while Bob listened patiently. 'And now he's got Verity back he doesn't want me at all.'

'I'm truly sorry, Gen,' said Bob when she had finished. 'I only wish there was something I could do to help.'

'Just listening did that.'

'Try to hold on to the knowledge that loving another person enriches life whatever the outcome.

We might resent it; we might fight against it, but ultimately our lives would be poor things indeed without it. Love is a very special thing, Genista.'

'I know.'

'My apologies for breaking up such a delightful scene. If I'd known you were having a tête-à-tête in my kitchen, Bob, with my wife, I would have knocked. I haven't been a husband for long enough yet to know the subtleties attached to the relationship, so you'll have to forgive my crassness. Did you bring the papers?'

Luke walked into the kitchen, completely ignoring Genista. He had shaved and was wearing a different suit from the one he had been wearing the previous evening. Love for him melted Genista's bones. She wanted to go to him and be taken in his arms more than she had wanted anything else in her life, but he was looking at her with a cold fury which left her in no doubt that her feelings were not reciprocated. It was on the tip of her tongue to remind him that his accusations were little short of ridiculous when he had just spent the night in Verity's arms, but all at once the effort was too much for her.

'I'm going upstairs,' she said unsteadily, then turned to Bob. 'I'll remember what you said,' she told him, smiling wanly. 'Tell Elaine to keep on fighting!'

She was sitting listlessly staring out of the window when the bedroom door crashed back and Luke strode into the room.

His fingers bruised her shoulders as he pulled her to her feet, shaking her as though she were a rag doll, until the room spun dizzily round her.

'You little tramp!' she heard him say thickly

through the ringing in her ears. 'How dare you entertain your lover here? Did you let him take you in my bed? Did you?'

She couldn't even raise the energy to protest at his rough treatment of her.

'What does it matter what I did?' she heard herself say wearily.

'You're my wife!' Luke gritted at her. 'That's what it matters, and Bob is one of my employees. Did you do it to get back at me, Genista? To punish me for the other night?'

If only she could float free of her body and escape from her pain, but it was impossible. Bruising though Luke's grip was, her body was unbearably aware of him. She felt a feverish need to reach up and touch him, to feel him tremble against her as urgently as he had done when he made love to her.

'Two can play at that game,' she heard him say harshly, and then she felt his hands on her back, tugging down her zipper, and exposing her body clad only in minuscule briefs and a lacy bra. She trembled as he sought the clip, and growing impatient wrenched at the dainty lace until it tore, revealing the soft thrust of her breasts to his probing eyes.

'Has *he* seen you like this?' he demanded harshly, 'touched you like this?'

His hands seemed to burn where they touched her skin. He seemed to be possessed of a primeval force that nothing could stem. For the sake of her self-respect she could not let him take her in revenge and anger, and yet as he thrust her down on to the bed, pinning her there with his superior weight, she could feel her will deserting her. The treachery of her body was searingly painful. There was no way she could meet the scorching triumph in his eyes as he cupped her breasts with his hands and she felt her nipples harden betrayingly against his palm. As though bent on punishing her further he teased the rosy peaks with his thumb, stroking roughly until she was almost mindless with pleasure, all the time watching her face with hard eyes.

This time she did not cry his name, nor did she try to prolong his touch. Deep down inside her self-disgust welled alongside longing. This was not how it should be, Luke using her body as though it were a toy, and watching her reactions like a voyeur. Her love rebelled, overcoming her desire. This was not how she wanted to remember their last encounter. She wanted her last memory of their lovemaking to be the mutually burning need which had brought them together before, not this calculated attempt to humiliate her by teaching her that he was her body's master.

'Satiated, are you?' Luke sneered cruelly. 'There'll be other times, Genista, when you won't be fresh from your lover's arms.'

'Go to hell!' Genista choked bitterly, hating him for a brief moment.

'If I do I'll make damn sure I take you with me,' Luke replied savagely. 'I'm not going to rape you, Genista. It will be much more subtle than that.'

'Save it for Verity,' Genista told him bitterly. 'You and she are both in the same league, and it's one which I'm thankful to say I don't aspire to!'

She heard him leave while she was still upstairs. He had left her without a backward glance. Going back to Verity, she imagined. He had probably only come home in the first place to warn her that he wanted her to leave. The scene she had just

endured must be the lingering effect of their first
meeting. He had dented his pride badly on that
occasion, and the need to be revenged still drove
him. Every time Verity teased him and left him
unsatisfied—and Genista suspected that she was
the kind of woman who would enjoy adopting such
tactics—would she be used as a substitute, a sex
object, taken without pity or love? She shuddered
deeply, then retched emptily and shivered with
mingled fear and nausea. She couldn't allow that
to happen, but if she stayed here there was no way
she could avoid it. She still loved Luke, and no
matter how strong her will when she was alone, he
only had to look at her for her bones to turn to
water, for all her resolve to fade and her treacher-
ous body to yearn for his touch.

She told Lucy she was going to London. The
girl's face dropped when Genista explained that she
could not take her with her. She packed mechanically, stowing her case in the boot of her
Mercedes, and bending to hug Lucy impulsively
before she climbed into her car.

She would ring Lucy from London to explain to
her that she wasn't coming back. It would be hard,
but far harder to tell her now, face to face.

The country road was virtually empty, but
Genista concentrated on her driving as she always
did. Later she was to reflect that her guardian angel
must indeed have been watching over her, but as
she took the fork which led to the motorway Luke
was occupying her mind to the exclusion of everything else.

She saw the child at the same moment as she
saw the lorry. She had only a split second to make
the decision—a moment of choice between the
safety of the child and the safety of herself—but

really it was no choice at all.

She heard the protesting screech of the lorry's tyres, felt the impact as she hit it head on, the sickening crunch of metal, the screams and then the silence punctuated only by the thin, high sound of a child crying. Not her child, please God, she prayed hazily as she fought against the beating wings of darkness, and for the first time in her life felt consciousness slip away.

CHAPTER NINE

'YOU'RE a very lucky young woman,' the doctor pronounced cheerfully, lifting her wrist and taking her pulse. 'That's what comes of driving a sensibly built car, I suppose. Had you been behind the wheel of one of those sardine cans that pass for modern cars, I doubt you'd be lying here all in one piece. That was a very brave thing you did,' he added a little more gently, 'and a certain six-year-old has you to thank for her life.'

Genista was lying on a trolley in the casualty ward of the hospital the ambulance had brought her to following the accident. A nurse had come to assure her briskly that she was not to worry. Someone had taken away her clothes and handbag and now she was lying on this narrow, high bed, dressed in a hospital gown, while the young casualty doctor prodded and poked.

'Doctor . . .' At her hesitant tone he stopped examining the bruises beneath her ribs where her seat-belt had tightened and looked up at her.

Genista licked her lips nervously. From the

moment she regained consciousness one thought
had possessed her to the exclusion of everything
else.

'I think I might be pregnant,' she said huskily.
'Will I . . . the baby . . .'

'How long?' the doctor asked her quickly. When
Genista told him, he relaxed a little. 'You might
just be lucky,' he told her frankly. 'Another few
weeks and I would say that a shock such as the
one you've just sustained would almost definitely
bring on a spontaneous abortion, but because your
pregnancy has only just started you could be
okay. We'll keep you in for a few days, just to be
on the safe side, though. Try not to worry.'

That was easier said than done, Genista thought
half an hour later, as the nurse made up a bed for
her in the women's ward.

'Try not to worry,' the girl comforted her, unconsciously echoing the doctor's words. 'Your
husband should be here soon. Sister has been in
touch with him.'

'Luke!' Genista's stomach muscles contracted
painfully. She had forgotten that the hospital
would contact him as her next of kin. Would he
realise that she had been leaving him? And if he
did would he be glad?

She realised that the drink the nurse had given
must have contained some sort of tranquilliser, for
minutes after she had finished it a numbing drow-
siness came over her.

'Try and sleep,' the nurse advised her. 'It will do
you good—you and your baby. It's nature's most
effective cure.'

When Genista woke up she was conscious of
various aches and pains all over her body from her
bruises. There was a screen round her bed, and she

could smell roses. She turned her head slowly, wincing a little at the pain from her jarred spine. There was a huge vase of red roses beside her bed, and sitting motionless in the chair next to it was Luke.

'How do you feel?'

It seemed to Genista that he was under a great strain. No doubt Verity had not been pleased when he left her to come to the hospital, but he was the type of man who would insist on carrying out what he considered to be his duty.

'The police tell me you had a lucky escape,' he added.

A muscle twitched in his jaw, and Genista watched it hazily, wondering if, for one moment, when they brought him the news, he had wished that fate had decreed otherwise.

'The lorry driver was full of praise for your quick thinking. You know you could have been killed?'

'I couldn't save my own life at the cost of that little girl's.' Weak tears slid down her cheeks, as her hands moved unconsciously to hold her flat stomach with protective fear.

'The doctor tells me you're pregnant.'

The emotionless words gave her no clue as to his own thoughts. The child she was carrying might have had nothing at all to do with him, to judge from his distant manner.

'I take it you want to keep the child.' He was studying the roses next to her bed, not looking at her at all. Red roses, Genista thought bitterly; a sop to convention, exactly the sort of flowers the nurses would expect a man to bring to the wife who had narrowly escaped death and was carrying his first child.

'Yes.'

Her own voice sounded flat and dead. A whole world had been encompassed by that one small word, because having Luke's baby would catapult her into a new life.

'God, what a mess!' The bitter vehemence of the words brought Genista's head up abruptly. Luke was still pale, his jaw clenched in an anger which seemed to be directed more at himself than her.

'The doctor wants to keep you in hospital for a few days—to run a few checks and make sure that you're suffering from nothing more than severe bruising. Once he's pronounced you fit to leave I'm taking you home.' As though he anticipated her arguments he continued brusquely, 'I know you were leaving me, Genista—and why, but I'm not letting you go back to that apartment on your own.'

His insistence that she returned home with him was merely another sop to convention; another example of his determination to do the correct thing, no matter what the cost to himself or anyone else. He couldn't want her in his house—not now. Verity would be furious. And how could she herself endure the torture of living with Luke and yet knowing that all the time he longed to be with someone else?

'I can manage,' she protested. 'It's better this way, Luke.' Tears filled her eyes, her voice suspended by the huge lump of pain in her throat. 'I appreciate that you feel obliged to take care of me, but . . .'

'But you'd rather go to Bob, despite the fact that it's my child you're carrying, is that it?' Luke ground out furiously, leaving the chair to pace the narrow confines of the bed. 'No way, Genista,' he told her brutally. 'You're coming home with me, otherwise I'll tell the doctor that you're going back to an empty flat, and you'll find yourself staying here even longer.'

She didn't have the strength to argue with him. It was far easier simply to lie back and let him dictate to her. And anyway, deep down inside, wasn't there still a small spark of hope, flickering on despite the fact that it should have long ago been quenched? She was carrying Luke's child, and although she couldn't pretend to herself that he loved her the way he loved Verity, mightn't he ... Mightn't he what? she derided herself, her thoughts trailing to an abrupt stop. Mightn't he turn his back on Verity for the sake of a child he hadn't even known he had fathered? For the thought to even cross her mind was ridiculously romantic, and surely a recipe for disaster. What had love brought her to, that she was willing to contemplate such a union just to have Luke near to her?

When the bell went, signalling the end of visiting time, Luke paused by her bed, staring enigmatically down at her, a strange expression in his eyes ... almost as though he wanted to touch her but daren't. She was imagining things again, Genista told herself, letting her own love for him trap her into seeing what she longed to see. He bent his head and his lips brushed her cheek—the sort of caress any man might give his wife in public, but it wasn't the sort of kiss Genista wanted, and her lips trembled unhappily.

It was difficult adapting to hospital life, perhaps because she was not truly ill enough to appreciate the care. Jilly came to see her one afternoon, dropping gratefully into a chair.

'Mm, lovely!' she commented appreciatively, sniffing Genista's roses. 'No need to ask who those are from. Luke was in the office when the news came through—talk about seeing someone stripped of all their defences! He looked like a man who's just been told he's lost all that matters to him in life.'

Genista smiled mechanically. Poor Jilly—if only she knew the truth!

Jilly said nothing about the baby, and Genista did not mention it either. The doctor had assured her that the danger was over, but she wanted to keep the news to herself. She doubted that she would see much of Jilly once she parted from Luke. She could hardly call at the office!

Genista had another visitor later that afternoon. Jilly stayed only a few minutes and once she had gone Genista drowsed lazily, paying no attention as the click of high heels approached her bed.

'I want to talk to you.'

The voice and the familiar smell of Opium reached her at the same time. Her eyes flew open, her heart contracting in dread as she saw Verity staring down at her. The other woman was dressed in a blue silk two-piece, looking so elegant that Genista was not surprised to see the rest of the ward watching them covertly. In contrast she felt that she had never looked worse. The accident had robbed her of her normal energy. Her skin was pale from being indoors, her hair lacking in its normal vitality. Next to Verity she felt plain and dowdy.

'Quite the little heroine, aren't we?' Verity hissed contemptuously. 'Well, it won't work, you know. Oh, Luke will take you back out of a sense of duty—more fool him. But it won't last. Have you no pride?' she demanded. 'Can you honestly contemplate sharing the bed of a man who you know wants to be with someone else? Oh, I know you love him! But if you think you have any chance of keeping him you're a fool. You might love Luke, but he loves me, and if you had any self-respect you'd make sure he wasn't forced into the situation of telling you so himself!'

For a long time after Verity had gone Genista lay staring into nothing.

Verity was right: she must refuse to go back with Luke. It would be better for both of them!

He had visited her every evening, and as the fingers of the clock crept round towards visiting time Genista's tension increased. She would be firm, but cool. She would not betray by a muscle how much she longed to go home with him. She would remind him that she had not wanted to marry him, and that he had never pretended it was a proper marriage.

By the time the clock struck seven she had convinced herself that she would be able to persuade him that she was right. However, she had not bargained for the fact that he had brought Lucy with him—a Lucy who confided delightedly to Genista that her parents were flying over that evening and the three of them were to spend the rest of her half term in London, sightseeing.

It could not be purely coincidence that in Lucy's presence Luke seemed far less austere, Genista reflected. He laughed and teased the younger girl, and at one point his fingers touched hers as he leaned across her bed. Genista withdrew from the contact immediately, but Luke's hand covered hers, clasping it lightly and curling it into his palm. When they got up to leave he raised her fingers to his lips, kissing them briefly before telling her that the doctor had told him that she could leave the hospital in the morning.

'You'll have to take things easy for a few days,' he warned her. 'Mrs Meadows has agreed to come in full time until you're feeling better.'

If she had any real backbone, she'd discharge herself from the hospital before Luke came back, Genista remonstrated with herself after he had gone. But would it do any good? He seemed determined to take responsibility for her, and she, weak fool that she was, badly wanted the memory of these last few days with him. In another week she would be feeling much better, far more able to do what she knew she had to do.

Luke insisted that she sit in the back of the car. Getting into it brought back memories of the accident, and for a moment she thought she was actually going to faint, but then Luke was beside her, his arms closing round her as he held her comfortingly for a moment.

'Don't worry about it. It's only to be expected. The doctor warned me of the possible traumatic effect of being in the car, but it's something you'll have to face sooner or later.'

Luke was an excellent driver, and Genista felt quite safe, or so she told herself until they reached a junction and a careless driver shot out in front of them. Even though she was sitting in the back, she 'braked' automatically.

The car stopped suddenly, and through her nausea Genista heard Luke swear, before he climbed out and the door slammed.

She was shaking from head to toe, and made no attempt to resist when he opened the door and slid in beside her, taking her in his arms and cradling her as though she were a frightened child. It was heaven to be held so close to him, to feel the warmth of his body and smell its familiar sharp odour. Telling herself that she was a fool, Genista closed her eyes and clung ashamedly to the broad warmth of his shoulders, quivering under the soothing touch of his hands stroking down her spine. Burying her face in the open neck of his shirt was an automatic reaction, as was breathing deeply the clean, male smell of his skin. She wanted these moments never to end, but at last Luke put her away from him, his jaw clenching as he looked down at her.

'I'm a man, not a monk, Genista,' he told her harshly. 'We both know the danger of what we were just doing.'

He drove on without a word, leaving her to stare blindly out of the car window. Had his words been a subtle reminder that although sexually she might arouse him, his reaction was purely physical, and that it would be Verity· of whom he would be thinking if they actually made love?

While he garaged the car, she went upstairs, walking automatically into the room she had shared with Luke. Her case was on the bed, and seeing it reminded her of everything that had happened since she left. She started to unpack automatically, staring white-faced with shock into the wardrobe as she opened the door. Less than a week ago it had held Luke's suits, next to her dresses—now it was empty.

'I've moved my stuff out,' Luke told her evenly, walking into the room. 'In the circumstances—for both our sakes—I thought it better. If you want me, I'll be within call, and I hope you won't let what's happened between us prevent you from calling me if you need me, Genista. Whatever else I might be guilty of, my desire to do everything I can for you is quite genuine.'

'I know.' Her voice sounded husky and strained. She glanced at the large bed she had shared with Luke and would now be occupying alone, willing the tears not to fall.

'Why don't you lie down and have a rest?' Luke suggested. 'I'll bring you a drink.'

'I'm fine,' Genista replied automatically, and then remembered that he might want to talk to Verity. She owed it to him to be as unobtrusive as possible. After all, he could hardly *want* her company.

She was undressed and in bed when he came back with a cup of tea.

'If you want to go to the office . . .' she began, thinking to offer him an opportunity of leaving her, but he shook his head decisively,

'Work can wait. Whatever needs to be done I can do from here. I'm not leaving you alone, Genista. If you can't sleep, call me. The doctor gave me some sleeping pills for you.'

She pulled a wry face. 'No, thanks. I've had enough pills recently to last me a lifetime.'

It was not strictly true. She had been offered them, but had always refused, thinking of the child growing inside her. The nurses had understood and had not pressed, even on the nights when she lay awake until the early hours of the morning, dreading the emptiness of her future.

She dozed and woke late in the afternoon, breathing in the fresh country air through the open window. Downstairs she could hear a phone ringing and her stomach clenched. Was it Verity, ringing Luke?

To her surprise at seven o'clock he came upstairs with a covered tray which he placed beside her bed, and a bottle of wine.

'It's only an omelette,' he told her, surprising her further. 'I'm no chef, but Mrs Meadows couldn't stay this evening. You don't mind if I eat up here with you, do you?'

Mind? If only he knew!

The omelette was delicious and Genista had drunk two full glasses of wine before she realised it. She felt positively lightheaded; courageous enough to plead breathlessly with Luke to stay with her for another half-hour when he said that it was time she slept, but when he did eventually go she heard him leave the house and the sound of his car, driving away, and she knew beyond any doubt that pity was not and never could be enough!

Three days later she was up and about, pottering in the garden, and trying to keep out of Luke's way. He was still working from home, and she was meticulously careful about avoiding him. Her earlier euphoria about being home had been dissipated by the feeling of strain which now engulfed her. Living in the same house as Luke, but as distant strangers, was taking far more toll of her fragile reserves than a clean break would have done. In her apartment at least she would have been able to give way to her emotions, safe in the knowledge that her weakness would not be observed, but here she felt as though she were walking a tightrope from which she would inevitably fall.

Matters came to a head one afternoon when Luke had been shut in the library since early morning. Genista went out into the garden and walked aimlessly among the flower beds, before returning to the house to change for dinner.

With pain in her heart she selected a simple jersey dress from her wardrobe in a soft shade of green, which complemented her colouring. Clad in briefs and a dainty bra, she was just applying her make-up when Luke knocked, walking in before she could reach for her robe.

His abrupt, 'I must talk to you,' sent shivers of apprehension quivering down her spine, but she tried to school her features into polite enquiry, praying that she would not betray the sickening sense of dread spreading through her.

'We can't go on like this,' he told her brusquely. 'It's just not going to work out. I know you want to keep the child, and as it's my responsibility I shall want to provide for it. Oh, I know you can manage on your own, but . . .'

'But it would ease your conscience,' Genista supplied bitterly. 'There's no need, Luke. I'm keeping the child because I want to. It's a personal decision, which doesn't involve you. As you said, financially I can manage very well. I shall probably sell the apartment and buy a small house in the country.' Strange how the words formed themselves to make sensible sentences, ideas she had not even known she had coming logically from lips that felt numb with pain. 'It won't take me long to pack. I could leave almost straightaway.'

Luke made a negating gesture, his face bleak. 'Whatever you wish. I have to go away on business myself tonight—something which has just cropped up. I'll be gone several days, so there's no rush. All I ask is that you leave me your address, Genista . . .'

'There's no need,' she heard herself saying lightly. 'I shall keep on the apartment for a while, until I decide what I'm going to do, and afterwards (they both knew that she meant after the birth), I can't see any point in maintaining contact. You will have your life, and I shall have mine.'

'If that's what you want.'

If it wasn't all so hurtful it would almost have been funny, Genista reflected later, when Luke had gone. She knew he had gone, because she heard the car drive away. Had he gone to Verity? To tell her that soon he would be free?

She had told him she would leave straightaway, but suddenly she lacked the energy to do so. Her car had been returned and was in the garage, but she could not contemplate driving it. She would wait until the morning, she decided, and hire a taxi to take her to the station. Once she was in her own apartment she could start making proper plans for her future—a future which she had to keep reminding herself no longer held Luke.

In the event the taxi firm were heavily booked and unable to collect her until the afternoon. She checked the time of the trains and estimated that she would arrive in London during the evening. With her cases packed and time hanging heavily on her hands, she walked through the rooms which had been her home for such a short span of time, storing up memories for the long, lonely years ahead.

The taxi had been booked for two-thirty, and when, shortly after one, she heard a car, she thought there had been some mistake. She was poised at the top of the stairs, ready to descend, when the door burst open and Luke strode into the hall. He looked up at the precise moment that Genista looked down, dizzily trying to comprehend that what she was seeing was real and not merely feverish longing.

'Luke!'

His face paled when he saw her.

'I forgot something,' he told her brusquely. 'I thought you'd be gone.'

'I couldn't face the drive, so I decided to go by train. The taxi couldn't pick me up until two-thirty.'

Seeing him like this, just when she was on the point of taking herself out of his life for ever, was the cruellest blow she had yet endured. The sight of his dark head, his body encased in the immaculate business suit, made something snap inside her. The stairs seemed to shimmer and move below her. She blinked, trying to focus, and swayed, reaching dizzily for the banister. The small sound of protest in her throat alerted Luke. As the stairs rushed up to meet her, he dropped his briefcase and started to run. She felt herself falling and cried out fearfully.

'It's all right, you're quite safe.'

Luke's arms closed round her, the soft wool of his suit beneath her cheek, his voice rough and uneven.

'Let me get you back to the bedroom.'

She felt him lift her, carrying her to the room they had shared for such a brief span of time. The dizziness was gone, but her pulses still pounded, although this time it was not with fear. Luke bent to lower her on to the bed, and all at once his expression changed, his face bitter with a pain that made Genista catch her breath.

'Oh God, Genista!' she heard him mutter hoarsely against her hair. 'I can't let you go. Don't ask me to, I beg you. I give you my word I won't lay a finger on you . . . won't do anything you don't want me to do. We'll start all over again, I promise you, and this time . . .'

She must have made a sound, because he

suddenly released her, turning his back on her to stare out of the window. 'I didn't come back because I'd forgotton something,' he told her abruptly. 'I came back because I had to see this room once more; to try and imprint on my mind the memory of you in it, in my bed—in my arms. God knows I've given you good reason to hate and despise me,' he went on. 'First I took your virginity; then I gave you a child. You'd think pride alone would keep me away from you when I know how you feel about Bob—didn't I hear you tell Lucy with my own ears how you felt about love? But none of it makes any difference. I only have to look at you and I ache for you. I fell in love with you the moment you walked into Greg Hardiman's flat. Until that moment I'd never believed in love at first sight. I was bored, on the point of leaving, when suddenly you walked in and and it was as though I'd been struck by a bolt of lightning. I took one look at you and knew. And you looked back. In my arrogance I thought you felt the same. My feelings for you were so intense that I couldn't believe you weren't feeling them to.

'Then you gave me that brush-off. I wanted to hate you, to hurt you as you'd hurt me, and then I found out that you were the girl Greg had told me was having an affair with Bob. I nearly went mad with jealousy. I couldn't bear to think of him looking at you, touching you . . . I had to take you away from him, so I forced you into marriage. I told myself that in time you would come to love me. You *had* to love me. That night when I made love to you, I thought I was going out of my mind. Every instinct told me that you'd never known any man, but I couldn't rely on my instincts. I knew you and Bob had been lovers! When I discovered the truth I could have killed myself. But I didn't.' His mouth twisted bitterly. 'Perhaps it would have been better if I had done, that at least would have been a quick death. This way, dying slowly inch by inch, hurts far more.

'Any decent self-respecting man would have set you free then, but I couldn't. I told myself I wouldn't touch you, that I'd wait and teach you to love me, but I couldn't stop myself from wanting you. I knew that forcing you to respond to me sexually would only increase your loathing of me, but it was the only way I could reach you, the only way I could make you come alive for me. Bob possessed your heart, and I told myself that possessing your body was some compensation, but it wasn't. I can't go on any longer, Genista. Bob is married and intends to stay married. So won't you give me a chance? I promise I won't so much as lay a finger on you unless you ask me to, I . . .'

Genista could bear it no longer. Luke had humbled himself enough, and listening to him she had run the whole gamut of emotions from sheer disbelief through pain to tear-filled joy as she heard him describe the emotions which up until now she had thought hers alone. Luke loved her!

He still had his back to her. She left the bed and walked up to him without making a sound, but some sixth sense must have alerted him. He turned towards her, his hands tightening on her shoulders with a pressure that bruised her bones as he held her away from him. If she had not believed his words, his face was sufficient to assure her that he was speaking the truth. It was the face of a man who has endured untold agony, and she longed to reach up and smooth away the pain.

'You said you wouldn't touch me,' she reminded

him gently, watching the immense self-control with which he withdrew his hands, clenching and unclenching his fingers as though the action brought him some measure of physical relief.

'Unless I asked you to.'

He turned away from her, and a quiver of pain ran through her. They had wasted so much time already, it seemed pointless to torment him now.

'Please touch me, Luke,' she begged hungrily, letting both her eyes and her voice betray her need. 'Take me, possess me, and make me whole again, because without you I simply can't function. You've taught me the true meaning of love, you've brought my body to full womanhood, and shown me things I never knew existed. I love you!'

The words were smothered beneath his mouth, his whole body shaking feverishly as he dragged her against him. For a moment neither spoke, content for the drugging, endless kiss to say all that needed to be said. Their clothes were an unbearable barrier which neither hesitated to remove, and Genista gasped once as she felt the driving force of the passion Luke had dammed up, and then she was joining him joyfully, urging him to show her that she was not merely dreaming.

He carried her to the bed and laid her on it tenderly, kissing her as he had done once before, with the same reverence that worshipped the perfection of her femininity, just as she gloried in his intense maleness.

This time there were no barriers. She was able to see so much that had been hidden from her before. Just as she had hidden her love from Luke so he had concealed his from her. Her body quivered in pleasure beneath his hand as she abandoned herself to his mastery, touching new pinnacles of pleasure,

her body so acutely sensitised to him that even the
lightest puff of breath aroused and enticed.

Her hands explored his body with a freedom she
had never allowed herself before, and with his possession came a pleasure that transcended everything that had gone before.

In its sweet aftermath she lay supine in his arms,
glorying in the heavy thud of his heart beneath her
ear and the sure knowledge that the pleasure they
had just shared had been mutually overwhelming.
It hadn't taken the hoarse words of love Luke had
muttered between his kisses, nor his brief triumphant cry at the moment of possession, to tell her
this; she had seen it in his face when he told her of
his suffering, and known that it had never been
and never could be merely desire which had
prompted his actions.

Jilly had been right after all. He had fallen in
love with her at first sight. The knowledge made
her feel humble and grateful that she had been
granted this second chance to seize the precious
gift she had wantonly spurned earlier through ig-
norance.

'I never loved Bob—not in the way you thought,'
she told him gently. 'But I daren't take the risk
that you might go to Elaine.' Quickly she told him
about Elaine's operation, drawing a soft groan of
self-anger from Luke's throat.

'I'll make it all up to you,' he swore huskily.
'When they told me at the hospital that you were
carrying my child, I could have killed Verity for
preventing me being at home to stop you leaving.'

Genista trembled. Verity! She had forgotten her!

Luke felt her stiffen and tilted her chin. 'What's
the matter?' he asked.

'Verity ... I thought you loved her,' Genista

mumbled. 'She came to see me. She told me you wanted to get rid of me . . .' Tears welled and fell, and were kissed away one by one, until the raging furnace which had turned to glowing embers in the aftermath of their lovemaking took fire again, and Luke's explanation had to wait upon a deeply passionate kiss which left them both trembling with the renewal of their desire.

'She got in touch with me when Philip went back to Marina,' he told her then. 'She told me she still wanted me; and subtly indicated that unless I played ball she would break up Philip and Marina a second time. I couldn't take that chance. I had to play along with her, even though I was loathing every moment of it. She knows the truth now.' His voice was very grim.

'But you loved her once.' The words had to be said, even though saying them drove them into her heart like sharp thorns.

'No.' Luke was emphatic. 'I wanted her, and very badly, but I was never under any illusions about what she was. She was the one who announced our engagement, and then when I refused to co-operate she turned her attention to Philip—something for which I've never really forgiven myself. I knew what she was like, I knew the sort of predator she was. I could willingly kill her for hurting you, though.

'Tell me you love me,' he demanded roughly. 'I still haven't heard you say it—not properly . . .'

'Funny,' Genista teased, 'I thought I'd managed to get the message over loud and clear!'

His sudden tension communicated itself to her, and she looked up, her heart beating swiftly at the expression in his eyes. She alone had the power to make this man look like this; to arouse his love and desire.

She lifted her hands to cup his face, revelling in the slight rasp of his skin against her palms.

'I love you, Luke,' she said softly, drawing his head down towards her, her lips parting tremulously in anticipation.

His harsh groan of satisfaction was stifled as their lips met. 'I don't intend to spend any more nights driving around the countryside for fear of what my longing for you might force me to do,' he told her huskily, banishing for ever the faint shadow that he might actually have accepted what Verity had so blatantly offered him. And to think that all the time she thought he was merely assuaging his love for Verity with her, when in actual fact . . . She drew a ragged breath, laughing a little at her own folly—at their joint folly.

'And the baby,' Luke said unevenly. 'I thought you must hate me and it—but the doctor told me how you'd begged him with your first words to tell you that you hadn't lost it.'

'It's your child,' Genista said simply, 'a part of you. A reminder that you had actually wanted me . . . loved me . . .'

They both heard the sound of car tyres on the gravel at the same time.

'The taxi!' Genista exclaimed in horror, clapping her hands to her mouth. 'I'd forgotten all about it!'

'Leave it to me,' Luke told her, reaching for his trousers. He smiled briefly as he reached the door. 'Don't go away, will you?'

'What will you tell him?' Genista asked.

Luke smiled again. 'I shall tell him that my wife is staying here—where she belongs,' he said softly. 'And then I'm going to come back and show her how much I love her—if she'll let me.'

Genista's smile held the radiance of a rainbow after rain. As he went downstairs she leaned back against the pillows, her fingers laced lightly across her still flat stomach. Luke's child! Her throat tightened with happy tears, and when Luke came back, she opened her arms wide to receive him, the past and its bitterness forgotten as together they re-avowed their love.

THE SPORT OF KINGS

Falconry, the art of using hawks to hunt small game, has long been regarded as the sport of princes and kings. It immediately conjures a romantic image of a man riding across country fields on horseback, one arm holding the reins, the other sheathed in leather and raised high, bearing aloft a hawk. The prey—a pheasant, partridge or quail—is flushed out. The rider raises his arm, and the hawk spreads his mighty wings and sails into the sky. Soaring high above the earth it fixes its sharp eyes upon the prey and then folds its wings and dives, snatching the small bird with its long talons and killing it instantly.

Only about a dozen species of hawks possess the characteristics that allow them to be trained by man, and the favorite is the peregrine falcon, which Genista spots hovering high in the sky above the English countryside. The peregrine is extremely rare today, endangered by those who trap them illegally (this bird fetches up to $30,000 on the black market!). People who train hawks are called falconers. And weeks of gentle patience are required before a falcon's training is complete.

Though falconry is an ancient sport dating back almost 3,000 years to the kings of ancient Assyria, today it is practiced in North America and Europe, and is also the favorite pastime of the oil-rich sheikhs of the Middle East. On a recent state visit to the Middle East, the prime minister of Canada greatly honored the king of Saudi Arabia by presenting him with a peregrine from Canada's North—one of the last frontiers for falcons existing in their natural habitats.

Legacy of
PASSION

BY CATHERINE KAY

A love story begun long ago comes full circle...

Venice, 1819: Contessa Allegra di Rienzi, young, innocent, unhappily married. She gave her love to Lord Byron—scandalous, irresistible English poet. Their brief, tempestuous affair left her with a shattered heart, a few poignant mementos—and a daughter he never knew about.

Boston, today: Allegra Brent, modern, independent, restless. She learned the secret of her great-great-great-grandmother and journeyed to Venice to find the di Rienzi heirs. There she met the handsome, cynical, blood-stirring Conte Renaldo di Rienzi, and like her ancestor before her, recklessly, hopelessly lost her heart.

SUPERROMANCE

Longer, exciting, sensuous and dramatic!

Fascinating love stories that will hold
you in their magical spell till the last page
is turned!

Now's your chance to discover the earlier
books in this exciting series. Choose from
the great selection on the following page!

Choose from this list of great

SUPERROMANCES!

SUPERROMANCE

Complete and mail this coupon today!

- -

Worldwide Reader Service

In the U.S.A.	In Canada
1440 South Priest Drive	649 Ontario Street
Tempe, AZ 85281	Stratford, Ontario N5A 6W2

Please send me the following SUPERROMANCES. I am enclosing m
check or money order for $2.50 for each copy ordered, plus 75¢ to
cover postage and handling.

☐ # 8 ☐ # 14 ☐ # 20
☐ # 9 ☐ # 15 ☐ # 21
☐ # 10 ☐ # 16 ☐ # 22
☐ # 11 ☐ # 17 ☐ # 23
☐ # 12 ☐ # 18 ☐ # 24
☐ # 13 ☐ # 19 ☐ # 25

Number of copies checked @ $2.50 each = $_____
N.Y. and Ariz. residents add appropriate sales tax $_____
Postage and handling $_____.75
TOTAL $_____

I enclose_____.
(Please send check or money order. We cannot be responsible for cash
sent through the mail.)
Prices subject to change without notice.

NAME_____
(Please Print)
ADDRESS_____APT. NO._____
CITY_____
STATE/PROV._____
ZIP/POSTAL CODE_____

Offer expires May 31, 1983   30156000000